LOVE ON THE MALECON

Love on…
Book One

Aubrey Parr

This novel is purely a work of fiction. Any characters, names, or events are the product of the author's imagination. Any resemblance to real persons, places, or events is purely coincidental.

Dedication:

This book is dedicated to...

Katie – For keeping me writing so she could keep reading.

and

Kelly – For seeing me as a writer from the beginning.

PROLOGUE

"He just walked out! Good riddance to him then!" Nicole was practically yelling now. She held the phone to her ear with her shoulder. She was throwing clothes into a suitcase, barely noticing what she chose. She knew that Kate was going to try and calm her down. That's what she always did. Kate was far more even keeled than Nicole. That's probably why their friendship had lasted for so many years; they balanced each other out.

"Breathe, Nic," Kate reminded her, "You just got back from the funeral. You need to just take some time for yourself."

Oh, done! Nicole thought to herself. She wasn't ready to tell anyone, even Kate, that she had booked a ticket to Puerto Vallarta. Well, anyone but Andrew. And look how that turned out. He just left.

CHAPTER ONE

It was the first open-ended plane ticket that Nicole James had ever purchased. It came with a return flight, of course, but somehow this felt more like a one-way trip. She had just buried her father and this seemed like the best tribute to his life. It was the least she could do since she didn't get to say good-bye.

As soon as she had found out that she hadn't made it to him in time, she knew what she wanted to do. Booking the flight was the easiest decision she had made in a long time and it felt like the right one. It didn't come without its risks. Her editor at Chicago Home Magazine was not thrilled with the last minute extension to her time off. Then again, when someone's father dies, one is usually given a little more leniency.

There was also Andrew to consider. He chose to skip the trip with her and Nicole took that as a bad sign for their relationship. The heap of self-help and relationship books that weighed down her carry-on bag was going to help her figure out that situation. Andrew didn't even know her return date wasn't booked. No one did. Two weeks sounded like a nice length of time but she wasn't ready to commit just yet.

The pilot came over the intercom and informed the passengers that they were starting their descent into Puerto Vallarta. She smiled at the thought of the 90-degree temperature that waited for her below. It had been years since she had been to Mexico. Her father's work had taken him around the globe several times over the past decade and he had always said that Puerto Vallarta was his heaven on Earth. Nicole wondered if her father's heaven was really made up of cobblestoned streets, little restaurants, and a Malecon- the stone seaside walkway- he could stroll for all eternity.

Her head started to spin again at the thought of her father. She was not prepared for his death. Although suffering a slow death would have been awful, Nicole couldn't help but think that some forewarning would have been nice. But accidents don't work that way. Still, she would have loved to spend a few minutes with him by his hospital bed to have some closure. There are so many things that she would have said. But he had been too far gone. Even if they were in the same city, she still may not have made it to the hospital in time. No plane would have been fast enough, but she still had to try. She lost her mother so young. It had been the two of them for as long as she could remember. Now, one careless decision made by a stranger driving a car had taken her father from her.

Lost in her thoughts, Nicole barely noticed that the plane had touched down.

"We landed dear. You can relax," the elderly woman next to her said as she patted her hand. Nicole didn't remember grabbing onto the arm rest.

"Oh, thank you," she smiled, adding a half-hearted laugh.

As Nicole sat there in a daze, waiting for her turn to disembark, her thoughts turned to Andrew. Andrew Hanson was the complete opposite of her previous boyfriends. Nicole always had a thing for bad boys and too many had broken her heart by the time Andrew walked into her life. A complete change was just what Nicole thought she needed.

He was a lawyer and certainly looked the part. His chestnut brown hair was always just so and his suits were always immaculately pressed. He was classically handsome with tanned skin and blue eyes. His nose was perfect and he had a sweet smile. She admitted to her friend Kate once that he kind of reminded her of a Ken doll. She was a little scared that it wasn't a compliment. And though she had never witnessed it, she suspected that he even ironed his jeans. Another mystery was his tan. He was tan year-round and they lived in Chicago. How was that possible? Was he hiding a membership to a tanning salon along with the closet jeans ironing?

Andrew never seemed to be entirely comfortable in his own skin. And although she loved him dearly, he was a little too stuffy for Nicole at times. Nicknames made no sense to him. He didn't even use terms of endearment. He never liked it when anyone tried calling him Andy. In his eyes, that was not his name. Nicole was simply Nicole.

He was sweet and gentle, in his own way. They went to fabulous dinners at nice restaurants and he indulged her love for the theater. Though she appreciated those things, she loved the casual side of life as well and there was still the part of her that missed hanging out in a hole-in-the-wall pub or a beach bar. She laughed to herself at the thought of Andrew walking into a grungy dive. He'd probably wipe down the barstool with hand sanitizer before sitting down.

Their last conversation had been short. She told him that she needed a vacation and wanted to visit her father's favorite place on Earth as a tribute to his life. That was all she was able to say before "no" came out of Andrew's mouth. Nicole wasn't sure if he was saying that he didn't want to go or if he was really trying to tell her that she wasn't allowed to go herself. As if she was a child asking permission. She didn't wait to find out the answer. She told him to leave their apartment while she packed and he had left without any other communication.

Nicole replayed the short scene over and over in her head. She couldn't quite believe how quickly he had walked out. How could it have been so easy for him? She wasn't even sure he knew where she had gone. Sure, she had told him numerous times that Puerto Vallarta was her father's favorite place. But would Andrew remember?

Nicole also surprised herself at how easy it was for her to board a plane without her boyfriend of three years having any idea where she was headed. Frankly, she liked the idea that she was unreachable. She wasn't even sure she would turn her phone back on now that they were on the ground. Her only family left was gone. Her friends were grown adults with lives to lead. Everyone could survive a hiatus without reaching her. No one could blame her for disappearing for a bit and soon enough everyone would know she was okay. Well, no one could blame her but Kate.

Kate was her matter-of-fact, hilarious, there-for-you-no-matter-what type of friend. Not letting Kate know her whereabouts would be inexcusable in Kate's eyes. And she could keep Nicole's secret from Andrew if needed. She reminded herself, yet again, that it was only two weeks, right? Then that sneaking suspicion popped back in her head, the one that told her that this felt like a one-way trip. She brushed it off, attributing it to her state of mourning. Surely she wasn't quite in her right mind at the moment.

Nicole's back began to ache even more as it was finally her turn to head up the aisle. As she stepped off the plane onto the platform, the sunshine was a smack in the face, like a splash of cold water awakening her from her haze. She was there. She had made it.

She immediately thought of her father. She was happy and sad all at the same time. Nicole imagined old Bill's face, the mischievous smile he would have as he would set foot in his favorite place on Earth. Images of her father filled her head, from as far back as she could remember to the last moments she had spent with him. Maybe that was his way of telling her that he was there with her. She took a deep breath and smiled at the idea of that.

All of the passengers filed down the stairs and piled into a waiting bus to take everyone to baggage claim and customs. Luckily, she was one of the last to board the bus and the entire process at the airport was actually rather quick. It seemed like a nice start to her trip.

Her taxi pulled up to the Playa Vallarta hotel. It was right in the middle of the Romantic Zone of Puerto Vallarta. Nicole had been to Mexico before but she had always stayed in Cancun at a variety of huge resorts. This trip was all about her father. She wanted to experience his Puerto Vallarta. She wanted to stay at his favorite hotel, frequent his favorite bars, and eat at his favorite restaurants. One of her favorite stories was hearing about when he met the owner of The King's Head pub down the street from his hotel. It was a British pub in the middle of Mexico. The owner had spent his "holiday" in Puerto Vallarta, returned to

England, and sold all of his belongings to come back to open the pub. Nicole always thought that was such a fun story and she couldn't wait to visit and hear it for herself

She immediately felt her father's presence in the Playa Vallarta and fell in love with the place right away. There was an open air lobby with trees inside. Just past the desk, tables spilled out from the restaurant. There was a large lobby bar and a swimming pool, all before an entrance to the beach. It wasn't a huge hotel like so many of the resorts in Mexico can be. Though Nicole had always been drawn to the all-inclusive resorts where you didn't have to leave the property, in this very moment, she couldn't figure out why.

Playa Vallarta was quaint, clean, and inviting. It made her feel like she would be a guest, not just a number. She had begun to pull her suitcase behind her when a little man in a crisp white summer suit came up and took it from her.

"Please allow me to assist, señorita. My name is Hector and I will be here for you, mi amor." Nicole smiled and let him help with her bags. He was so little and absolutely adorable. It seemed as though someone had stuck a normal sized man in the dryer and shrunk him just a hair. He had kind eyes and a bright, happy smile. Nicole knew instantly that they could be friends.

"Thank you," she smiled, "I'm hoping to get checked in quickly so that I can relax a bit after my trip."

Hector nodded in agreement, "Of course, señorita, I will make certain you are assisted immediately."

He waited patiently for her to check in and then showed her to the elevators. As she followed Hector, Nicole noticed the beautiful color of the wood in the lobby bar- brilliant tan with bands of orange that sparkled in the refection of the sun. It was huge, with a thick elbow rest, and seemed to go on forever. There was a heavy overhang above, in the same amazing colors, with beautifully colored glasses dangling from it. Each style of glass was a different color and made Nicole want to order all kinds of fun mixed drinks with umbrellas in them. There were plants placed randomly all around the shelves above with vines hanging down that added a natural warmth to the area. There were a few guests scattered around the bar, some in bathing suits, taking a break from the sun.

Nicole was wondering which barstool would have been her father's when she noticed a man sitting there, aimlessly stirring his drink. She felt a chill all over as she realized he had been watching her. He looked like he was most likely American, maybe forty, with salt and pepper hair. (Why was it that a man could become more attractive when he grayed but it just made women look old?) His face was angular with a sharp jaw line and it looked as though if he didn't get up the energy to shave in a few days, he would officially have a beard. So far that may have been her favorite thing about him. She loved everything from a five-o'clock shadow to a full-on beard; it made a man look rugged and exciting. He was in a casual t-shirt and tan linen pants with flip flops dangling off his feet. He looked like he had just come from a walk along the beach. Her heart skipped a beat when she saw edges of tattoos that were peeking out from beneath both sleeves of his t-shirt. Nicole loved tattoos; she had a few small ones as well. She preferred meaningful little accents for herself but with men, the more the better. Andrew didn't have any tattoos. And no matter how many times she suggested he consider one, he wouldn't budge.

They made eye contact. He had searing dark eyes that seemed to look right inside of her. He tipped his glass to her as a hello and looked at the empty chair next to him. His expression didn't change; he just stared at her with an intensity that she'd never felt before. Nicole decided to continue their silent communication. She pointed to the elevator and then back to the chair next to him and smiled. He seemed to understand that she wanted to go upstairs to freshen up from her travels and then would join him at the bar. His eyes never left hers but he did reveal a little smirk on his face as she finally pulled her attention back to Hector and the open elevator that waited for her.

Not wanting to take too long, Nicole flew through a shower and put on one of the dresses she had in her suitcase. She did a quick inventory of what she had remembered in her hasty packing. There were a handful of dresses and skirts, a few pairs of light summer pants and shorts, a pile of tank tops ranging from casual to dressy, two bathing suits, flip flops, and some bras and underwear. Luckily she had remembered to pack some running gear and her shoes. Not too bad. She could work with this and buy anything else she might need along the way.

After swiping on some mascara and lip gloss, she stepped back from the mirror to survey the results. Her long blonde hair was wet from the shower but she was one of those lucky girls who could let her hair naturally air dry and look like she had spent time styling it that way.

Nicole always felt that she was the girl-next-door type of pretty. By no means did she think that she was some grand beauty but she knew what her assets were and did her best to accentuate them. She had always been told that her eyes and lips were the best features, so mascara and lip gloss were essentials. She had fair skin that didn't really need much added to it. She was tall and leggy with a little more curve than she would prefer. Though men seemed to like the curves, Nicole always wished for a little less.

She had chosen a very casual tan summer dress so that it wouldn't look like she was trying too hard. She threw on one of her black bathing suits underneath, so she had an excuse to be downstairs in case she had misunderstood their little silent conversation. Satisfied with the reflection in the mirror, she stepped back and noticed some of the relationship books that she had brought with her. What was she doing? She lived with Andrew and though they were fighting when she left, he was still her boyfriend. Grabbing her purse, she figured she could start reading those books tomorrow and she headed for the door.

CHAPTER TWO

Derek Stone was sitting in his regular spot at the Playa
Vallarta bar. He had just finished running over some
numbers at the sister hotel, Paraíso, across the street.
The hotel name meant "Paradise" and it was just that.
The busy season had been good to them and now things
were quieting down. Though Derek had ownership in
the Paraíso, he still favored the bar at Playa Vallarta. He
had been sitting in that same barstool when he made a
decision that had changed everything for him, so he had
a soft spot for the place.

Derek had been a Mixed Martial Arts fighter
almost fifteen years ago, in what felt like another life.
Derek was a good fighter; it came easily to him.
Outside of the fighting cage, he had grown into a rather
laid back man, quite different from when he was a kid.
Derek grew up without a father in the Detroit area and
his mother wasn't much to speak of. So for the better
part of his life, Derek had taken care of himself. That
included fending for himself in whatever way possible,
which most of the time meant fighting. As a kid, he
made money to buy himself food and clothes by
fighting near the bike racks. As he grew, so had the
crowds and the venues. By the time he was seventeen
and fighting in warehouse basements for a thousand
dollars a pop, he was recruited by a man who
introduced him to MMA fighting and the Ultimate
Fighting Championship. With his natural abilities and
some training, the man had said, he could actually make
a career out of it. And so Derek's unfortunate start in
life had been preparing him for his first real job. Derek

was always able to channel his anger with his parents into the fighting cage and it never seemed to fail him. It wasn't long before he had won a rather large chunk of change.

When Derek was twenty-five years old, he decided to take a vacation to Mexico. He wanted to get away from all the hype of the fighting world. By no means was he a household name, but the UFC following was growing and he figured he could be recognized in a place like Cancun. He settled on Puerto Vallarta, which was a smaller, more authentic town, to relax. He had just come in from running on the beach when he sat down at the Playa Vallarta bar for a beer. A man had stopped at the bar to take a business call.

The man surely didn't think that Derek was of any consequence because he spoke freely in front of him. He discussed the area just north of Puerto Vallarta: Nuevo Vallarta. From what Derek could gather, Puerto Vallarta had been growing past capacity and expansion had already begun north with huge success. He figured investing in some land further north now would lead to a huge payday in the near future. It seemed like whoever was listening wasn't biting. Standing in front of Derek was an opportunity- a man with an idea who needed someone with the means to invest. When the man ended the call, he sat down next to Derek, looking frustrated and defeated. Without much more thought, Derek told the bartender to bring over two shots of tequila and introduced himself.

Given Derek's age and appearance, the man was apprehensive. He was Roger Long, a real estate developer. Roger became more receptive to the idea when he learned about Derek's fighting career and the winnings he would like to invest. They had talked for most of the afternoon. Derek had been ready to retire from his fighting career and move on. He had a large bank account from his winnings and there wasn't much motivation left to keep him going. Almost all of his frustration with his parents had been sorted out during the past five years in the UFC cage. Winning was nice but it wasn't enough. This seemed like the perfect plan: invest his money so that it would grow for him. He and Roger agreed to take a drive out to the location and have a true business meeting about it. Roger had all the contacts necessary in Mexico to actually make this happen but the laws were tricky, especially when you weren't a Mexican citizen.

Derek didn't have a fancy college degree nor did he pay much attention in high school. But he did have street smarts. He learned to trust his gut in life, to follow his intuition, and it had served him well. His intelligence showed in his fighting. He paid attention to his opponent's tells, he watched to see where fighters planted their feet before swinging or expressions they would make before certain attacks. He always thought he could just fight, not understanding that his brain took a part in the whole thing. Now he could turn that to his business investments.

The land the men invested in soon had a hotel built on it. The Samba Vallarta was a boutique-style hotel that was popular for the area. Part of Derek's criteria in the negotiations was that he be given living quarters on the site and a percentage of future revenue. He received one of the suites with a kitchenette and was always welcome to stay as long as he liked.

During the process, Derek had realized this industry could be a gold mine and he had no intentions of living in the States again. As soon as the Samba Vallarta was built and generating money, he began looking into new sites in other areas of Mexico. Predicting areas with growth potential, purchasing land before the expansion began, and then negotiating with hotel companies that desired the property seemed like such a simple idea. Kind of like the common place notion of "buy low, sell high." Derek seemed to have a gift for knowing the future. His gut was always right. One after another, Derek added more land and more hotels to his resume. Now here he sat at his favorite bar where it all began.

Then he saw her- an adorable leggy blonde walking up to the front desk to check in.

He tried not to date guests. It kept things simple. If he did take one of his hotel guests on a date, he never told her about his involvement. It was easier to be a guy on vacation from Detroit. He had recently also made the mistake of dating an employee. And of course Silvia happened to be a manager at the Playa Vallarta. Technically they were only a sister hotel to his, but he still should have known better. When Derek decided to end it between them, she wasn't very receptive to the idea. Luckily, nothing had gone past dirty looks and the occasional late night request to "talk." Derek had to admit that he wasn't sure how she'd react if she found out that he was taking out this blonde. She knew about his rule and he was definitely going to break it.

Even though the blonde had probably traveled all morning, she looked amazing. She was casual in a skirt and tank top, with her long hair pulled back out of her face. She smiled brightly and was nice to the employees. That was always something that Derek noticed. The "waiter test" went a long way in his book. Someone could be all smiles to you across a table in a restaurant, but how they treated the waiter told a lot about what type of person they were. When she turned from the front desk counter, he could see her gorgeous ice blue eyes. Without another thought, he tipped his glass to her and motioned for her to have a seat next to him. Somehow without a word exchanged between them, she let him know that she'd go up to her room and be back down for a drink.

Derek didn't get nervous, ever. He was an attractive guy, which served him well with women, and his career inside the fighting cage didn't allow for intimidation. He felt uncomfortable in situations involving families, purely because it was out of his element. But nerves? No, he didn't have a problem with them. Yet somehow his stomach knotted up at the thought of having this woman sit next to him. He took the time while she was upstairs to think about his past and how far he had come.

There were really only three occasions in his life that felt life-changing. The first time he got in a fight when he was a kid, when he discovered MMA fighting, and when he decided to invest in land in Mexico. He remembered the exhilaration he felt in all three of those moments. Derek realized that he just may be having one of those moments again. He didn't know what was going to happen but he could feel that something was going to change. And with that thought, he asked for a shot of tequila. The bartender, Emilio, gave him an odd look, given the time of day.

"Yes, this early. I need a bit of liquid courage." It hadn't occurred to him that it was before lunch and he was not known to drink alone at the bar in the morning.

He didn't want or need to get ahead of himself. Long term relationships, other than in business, were not a part of Derek's life. This woman, whoever she was, looked like fun and a nice escape from reality for a bit. Other than his failed attempt with Silvia, week-long relationships had been his norm. He was surprised at how many women seemed okay with casual sex and quick goodbyes. He knew how to wine and dine a woman while always letting them know that this wasn't going any further than the length of their vacation. He didn't feel like he was using anyone. They were all willing participants and he didn't lead them on. For his investments in areas like the Dominican Republic where most vacationers stayed on their resort for the entire visit, Derek would often spend time with his laptop by the beach or at the bar of other resorts. He had enough business connections and friends to allow him some perks at other resorts. That way, if he became interested in spending time with someone for the week, he was able to return back to his own resort each night or each morning.

He loved women, he just wasn't sure he had the skills to make a long-term relationship really work. Derek's current true love was his work. His tequila shot arrived and he swung it back quickly. Out of the corner of his eye, he caught a glimpse of Silvia. Of course she'd have to be there. She was going to need to get used to seeing him with other women. Vallarta was not a large city. Even if the blonde hadn't been staying at this hotel, there was still a chance that Silvia would see them out on the Malecon somewhere. She knew his favorite restaurants and he had noticed her frequenting them still.

Silvia seemed harmless enough; she just seemed like a girl that had a hard time moving on. She was young, cute and smart. One reason he decided to give dating a shot with her. They just didn't have much in common. They stopped having things to say to each other at a pretty alarming rate. And when he realized that he still wasn't comfortable letting her into his apartment at the Paraiso, he knew he wasn't willing to let the relationship go any further. He knew she resented it as well. He tried explaining that he was a private person and protective of his personal space but it wasn't enough.

His head was spinning a bit. He twisted his neck to one side until he felt it crack. It had always been a habit of his to help him relax. He cracked it the other direction, put Silvia far out of his head and, waited for the mysterious woman to arrive.

CHAPTER THREE

When the elevator door opened, she saw him sitting there, chatting with the bartender, and immediately ten different things that bothered her about Andrew popped into her head. It had to be a defense mechanism, a way of making herself feel better. She reminded herself that she loved Andrew and that this was only an innocent drink. This trip was her time away to escape from everything and an attempt to connect with her father's memory. She shook the feeling off and walked over to the bar.

He hadn't seen her get off the elevator so she sat down next to him. "Well, hello again," she said with a smile. She could see he was glad she hadn't changed her mind about their drink together.

"How was your flight?" he smiled, "What can I get you?" She asked for a beer and he ordered them each one along with two shots of tequila. "Figured we should start your vacation off right," he said with a smirk in his eyes. "I'm Derek."

"The flight was far too early," she said with a sigh. "I'm Nicole."

"Are you waiting for anyone to arrive?" he asked casually.

She considered how to explain why she was there. "My father spent a lot of time in Puerto Vallarta and this was where he always stayed," she continued to check out the hotel as she explained. "I just want to feel closer to him," she added with a bit of a wince as it was all too real that he was now gone.

"I'm sensing it was recent," Derek stated, but it seemed like he knew not to push any further.

"Yes," she admitted and then picked up the shot glass in front of her, "And on that note, let's do this and start my vacation."

After being with Andrew for years, there had been little for them to talk about lately. So these days, she loved meeting new people. She loved discovering another's life and the feeling when they both had so much to say. She especially loved those first conversations where each person is practically interrupting all the time because they each have so much to tell the other. The feeling like they would burst if they didn't explain everything immediately. She was getting a little bored with the silence at home and only the sound of the radio or television as she and Andrew sort of co-existed. It seemed blaringly obvious now. Had she really not noticed it before?

As she and Derek began to chat about the basics, Nicole noticed everything about him. Even though he was sitting, he looked like he was just under six feet tall and in extremely good shape, lean with just the perfect amount of muscle. She couldn't help but admit to herself how incredibly attractive he was. He looked like he could kick someone's ass if needed, which she found extremely sexy. She had always guessed that being raised mainly by her father fed into her love of bad boys. Her father himself had not been the type of man you would mess with. He wasn't a really large man, but he could command the attention of a room. His numerous tattoos from different parts of the world added to his tough appearance. Nicole always knew that he would do whatever it took to protect her. She was attracted to the same type of man, someone that would love her unconditionally and always protect her.

Derek definitely looked the part. She particularly loved his arms. He had strong forearms and his t-shirt tugged just slightly at his biceps. She got a closer look at the edge of his tattoo. It looked like some sort of design, but not the tribal art that was so popular these days. This looked like the work of a true artist. She blushed a bit when she realized that she was imagining his shirt off and his arms around her. And then she noticed his lips…

She had to stop herself and get back into the conversation before he thought she was a mindless bimbo. She couldn't exactly explain to him where her mind wandered, that she could practically feel the warmth of his body on top of her…

She had gathered that he was from Detroit and that he was some kind of real estate investor. She told him a little bit about growing up in the suburbs of Chicago. Their lives were very different but they had both been mainly raised by one parent. Nicole lost her mother to cancer at eight years old and he never knew his father. The one thing she could tell, though he said little about it, was that her father had been a far better parent than his mother. Both of them were only children and neither had been married.

"Look at that beach," Nicole said, staring out over the water, "I cannot wait to get out there for a run."

"You're a runner?" Derek stated more than asked.

"Well, no plans on ever running a marathon," she joked. "But I love the time outside. It's my version of yoga."

"Stress relief and meditation, huh?" he agreed.

"Exactly," she replied with a smile.

"We should go for a run while you're here," Derek mentioned casually.

Nicole loved that he was planning on seeing her again. "It's a date."

She realized that she hadn't had anything to eat since before her flight and picked up a nearby menu. Derek casually reached for it. "Would you allow me?" he asked, "I know what's best here."

"Thanks, as long as there are no mushrooms."

Nicole admitted to herself that she kind of liked the take-charge way about him. He wasn't doing it to be controlling or because he thought she was helpless. He just wanted her to have the best meal possible. She liked that he seemed to care about something so simple involving her.

He ordered her the steak quesadillas. As he passed the menu to Emilio, the bartender, Nicole saw multiple scars on his hand. She couldn't help herself asking, "Did you used to work with your hands?"

He looked down at them as if he'd almost forgotten the scars were there. "I was a fighter once upon a time," he told her. "Started in the school yard and finished in a professional fighting cage. Not much difference between the two when it comes down to it." She ran her fingers across his knuckles, light and slow, as if she wanted to make sure the wounds had indeed healed. The moment she touched his skin, she felt a sudden charge and in a flash, she was transported to the bed in her hotel room. They were naked and he was on top of her. She could feel his lips dragging along her neck while he held her hands firmly over her head.

Nicole drew her hand back and caught her breath. She couldn't quite tell what Derek was thinking. He noticed that she was unnerved but she hoped he thought it was only the scars. She remembered being told once that sometimes when actors needed to play a very dominant role, they would take boxing lessons to help them appear more confident. She hadn't thought of the random fact again until that moment. Maybe that was why Derek seemed so able to protect her. He had years of experience in the fighting cage and the confidence that could only come from protecting yourself in fight after fight.

As Nicole finished up the last of her beer, Emilio brought a fresh one along with her quesadillas. Though she hadn't asked for it, she was thankful it was there. She offered a piece of food to Derek and piled some guacamole on her own before taking a bite. She hadn't realized how hungry she was until she smelled the steak and cheese in front of her. The only word she could muster up after the first taste was, "Wow!" The home-made tortillas were filled with cheese, onions, and peppers, and whatever the spice was on the steak was fabulous. The guacamole was fresh, with thick chunks of avocado. She finished the first piece as fast as she could without forgetting all of her table manners.

She and Derek continue to talk about all sorts of things. When he finally asked about a boyfriend, Nicole was confused about how to answer. She knew she wouldn't lie, that wasn't who she was. She realized that she really didn't know her status with Andrew. They didn't have a huge fight, they hadn't yelled or thrown things. No one said that it was over. However, here she sat in Mexico and Andrew didn't seem to care. That seemed rather final, just without the grand finale. Nicole figured that the best solution was to explain exactly what she was feeling. She gave Derek a quick summary of the last conversation with Andrew and simply stated that she wasn't exactly sure what her relationship status was at the moment.

Surprisingly, she was quite interested in Derek's take on her Andrew Dilemma. When she finished telling him that Andrew might not remember what her father's favorite place was, she could tell that Derek caught on to the fact that her boyfriend may have no idea where his girlfriend actually was. His face crunched in concentration, as if he was trying to wrap his head around that scenario in his own life or maybe trying to think of a nice way to say something.

"What is it?" she asked cautiously.

"Let's just say it would seem that your Maybe Boyfriend and I are two very different men."

CHAPTER FOUR

Derek was surprised that he had let Nicole out of his sight that night or the next day. They had continued to talk most of the first afternoon. At one point, they moved from the bar to the pool. They leaned back on lounge chairs, sharing another bucket of beer and talking about everything from movies to card games they liked to play. Derek couldn't remember the last time a woman had made him feel this way. There were so many times he'd be watching her as they talked, the way her dress hung over her thighs, and it took everything in him not to reach his hand over, slide it up between her legs and pleasure her until she called out his name. He could see glimpses of the little black bikini she was wearing under her dress and, God, he wished for the chance to rip it off her body.

They watched the sun sink into the ocean and Nicole looked so at peace in that moment. When she told him that she was going upstairs because she had been up so early that morning, he could see that she was genuinely tired. Ordinarily, he may have asked a woman to stay for one more drink, but something was different about Nicole. He wanted her to be happy. He wanted to protect her. If that meant she got a good night's sleep and he tossed and turned while she haunted his dreams, so be it.

That was exactly what happened. He could not get her out of his head. What little sleep he did get was filled with dreams of her in his bed. That part was nice but restless. He spent most of the night pacing the floors, grabbing at his head in an attempt to physically pull her out of it. Nothing was working. At least her trip was twice as long as the usual Vallarta vacation. Though he was happy to have the two weeks, he knew he was going to want more. Already he couldn't get enough of this girl and they had only spent a few hours together.

He didn't know what to think of the Maybe Boyfriend back home. He preferred the women he saw to be single but he wasn't a saint. He knew there had been boyfriends at home from time to time, though he drew the line at husbands. Yet the thought of another man touching Nicole infuriated him. The fact that they shared a bed together every night before this was more than he could handle. He couldn't imagine what man would ever let that woman get on an airplane without knowing where she was going. Why hadn't the Maybe Boyfriend come with her? Whatever the reason, Derek intended to dig deeper into the matter.

He made it through the entire next day by visiting the Samba Hotel in Nuevo Vallarta. He needed to get some distance, a bit of a distraction. But by the next morning, he was pacing his apartment at the Paraíso, trying to decide the best course of action. Getting on his plane and flying to his furthest property was probably the smartest decision. But he knew damn well it wasn't the one he'd choose.

Going for a run wasn't an option either. He had already gotten up at a ridiculous hour and run a few miles along the beach. He knew he wasn't about to lose a second of time with this woman, so working was the best way to try and take his mind off of her. She had promised him dinner on the Malecon that night, so he just needed to get through the day. He probably should have spent the night at the Samba. He could have come back just before dinner.

He wasn't keen on the idea of working in the Playa Vallarta lobby bar. He didn't want to come across like a stalker if he saw Nicole; she knew he wasn't staying there. Plus he was sure he'd get an earful from Silvia the next time he saw her. He cared even less what she thought now but he didn't want her bringing him down off his high from Nicole.

So where to work? Maybe he'd just hole up in his apartment until it was time to pick her up in the lobby. He still hadn't decided when his cell phone rang.

"Hello?" he snapped.

It was Gael, his right hand man. Gael wasn't what one would call an assistant but he was an employee. Derek had met him in his first few years in the business. Originally from Mexico, he had gone to college in the States. Gael was extremely versed in the real estate and land laws in Mexico and was doing random contract work for other hotels when Derek convinced him to work exclusively for him. He became indispensable to Derek and not a day went by when they weren't discussing some sort of business opportunity.

Now Gael was checking in to see if he'd finished his research into their latest plan. Of course he hadn't. Nicole's arrival in Vallarta had changed everything. Derek let him know that he had set aside the better part of the day to make a final decision. Hearing Gael's voice helped him get his mind back on track.

Derek really loved this part of his job- using his gut instinct to decide which property was going to be the most successful and ultimately most lucrative. He opened his email and browser and began looking into the company's vision for their expansion into the United States. They had been extremely successful in Mexico and now comfortable enough to branch out, but where? That's where Derek came into the picture. This was where he had a sixth sense for these things. It's not like he threw darts at a map. He did serious research and visited the area's sites beforehand. And his choices never seemed to fail.

Derek had been looking into ideas in South Beach, San Diego, Chicago, and Houston. His gut kept taking him back to Chicago but he had to admit that he was concerned that Nicole might be affecting his thinking right now. The hotel concept was a spa getaway style. The idea seemed initially far-fetched in Cancun but that's exactly what made it work. It was the only one of its kind in the area. Derek was able to drop South Beach and San Diego off the list rather quickly by following the same formula. With it narrowed down to Chicago and Houston, there were still many things to consider. He stayed focused on reviewing land and building options in both cities until his stomach wouldn't let him concentrate any longer. Work never failed him and it didn't seem long before he had made it through the entire morning.

Derek rummaged through his kitchen, looking for something to eat, and came up empty. It was a gorgeous day outside, so he decided to walk down to one of his favorite restaurants. As he walked along the main road through the Romantic Zone in Vallarta, he kept catching himself noticing all the dresses in the endless store windows on the way. He could picture each one on Nicole. Derek realized that he was already noticing which color and style would suit her best.

He stopped at the restaurant and grabbed a table outside. Since he was a regular, the hostess came out with his usual beer and chips and took his order. She was a cute little thing, always extra friendly with Derek. Today he didn't even take a second glance other than to say hello.

He munched on his chips and tried to think about work until his phone rang. Gael again. There was an opportunity in Chicago that seemed to magically pop up. A hotel in a great location was coming up for sale, extremely hush-hush. Derek had initially made the bulk of his money buying land and sitting on it for at least a year. He'd sell for a nice profit when a hotel company was looking for the right site. Over the years he began working with some of those same companies to find locations when they wanted to expand. He charged a rather large finder's fee and would still negotiate in the same "living quarters and percentage of revenue" deal.

Derek had been concerned all morning that his gut was telling him Chicago purely because of Nicole, but this had to be a sign. "Barring any unforeseen issues," he told Gael, "Chicago it is."

"Should I gas up the jet?" Gael inquired.

With only thoughts of Nicole in his head, Derek replied, "For yourself. I want you to handle the initial meeting." There was a momentary silence, so he continued, "You can handle this." It was the first time in their career together that Derek would take a step back and let Gael take the reins. He wasn't about to lose a minute in Vallarta with Nicole.

"I appreciate the faith," Gael responded, "I won't let you down."

"I'll be there with you in a few weeks to finalize everything." Derek smiled, thinking of a chance to see Nicole again. "I have someone I'd like to visit while I'm there."

Just as he ended the call he heard, "What has you smiling?" in a voice he would recognize for the rest of his life. He looked up and Nicole was sitting down at his table.

"A business opportunity. In Chicago of all places," Derek admitted. He was a bit worried that she would think he went looking for a meeting in her city, so he added, "I'm sending my second-in-command there in the next few days to start some negotiations."

"How great would it be if you'd get to have some business trips there?" she said, with genuine excitement in her voice.

"I'd bet I could find some reasons to stay longer," he teased, raising his eyebrow at her.

She smiled at him while she imagined him in her apartment. Not sure how to react she changed the subject.

"I walked out of that store next door and saw you sitting here."

"Well, I'm glad you came over. Would you like some food? The fish tacos here are excellent. They should be here any minute." he offered.

"Sounds perfect! Are you done with work for the day?"

"For you, love, of course I am." He wanted to make the most of his short time with her and figured playing hard to get wouldn't be the smart move.

Nicole blushed a bit, but it was covered up by the waiter arriving with their lunch. She asked him to bring her what Derek was drinking and picked up a taco. Derek loved how comfortable they already felt together. As he watched her, flashes of his dreams from the past two nights flooded his mind. He hoped their dinner would go well and that he'd be invited back to her room afterwards. He could even picture her in his apartment, something he had never done with any other woman. As crazily as he had been thinking, he was still going to try to keep that rule in place. He wasn't entirely sure why that was so important to him. But it was a rule he had never broken before.

God, he loved her laugh. He was telling her a random story and the more she laughed, the more he realized that he wanted to take her to a comedy club the first chance he got. He wasn't quite sure there was one in Puerto Vallarta. He planned to know by the end of the day.

When they finished their beers, Derek asked if she'd like to continue shopping.

"Do you want to come with me? I have a few on my list that my dad told me about, but I'm sure you know some great new places." It was just what he wanted to hear. Derek was hoping he could get her to try on a few of those dresses he had seen. He was prepared to buy her entire stores if it made her smile.

They wandered into the first place they came to. It was packed to the rim with Mexican glassware. Luckily, the aisles were tiny and he enjoyed the excuse to move in extra close to her. He stood behind her and she fit perfectly in his chest as they looked at different trinkets. All of a sudden, she gasped.

"Look at these!" she picked up one of the glasses from a set of tequila bottle and shot glasses. It was thick and swirled with gorgeous blues and greens. As she examined it, she mused, "It would always remind me of our first drink together- shots of tequila."

As she smiled at him, Derek looked at the store clerk, "Wrap this up for us, *por favor*."

"Oh, you don't have to do that," she protested.

"You're right, it's the perfect reminder of our first drink. Who knows, maybe we'll have a shot from it on all of our anniversaries." Wait, what was he saying? Anniversaries? Nicole just smiled at him and kept looking at the glass. He couldn't figure out what was going through her mind. That was a ridiculous thing to say and she didn't seem freaked out at all. Was she going just as crazy as he was? At least they'd be in good company together.

They wandered in and out of different stores on their way towards the Malecon. She let him buy her a few summer dresses. As they passed the flea market, the store attendants became more and more aggressive for their patronage. Derek began holding Nicole's hand and by the fourth or fifth stall, he had his arm protectively around her. Though he had always found the salesmen's incessant hounding rather annoying, this was the first time it bordered on harassment. When one man grabbed Nicole's arm to stop her, Derek almost ripped it off. She seemed a bit surprised by his reaction, but thankful. He could tell that she didn't want the man touching her either.

"Thanks," she said as they walked off to the sound of the man yelling at them in Spanish.

"Anytime, love. No one should ever touch a woman without her consent even if it was just to get you to shop in his store."

He gave her quick squeeze and he loved how she leaned her head against his shoulder as they continued walking. Giving her a quick kiss on the head, he led them toward a makeshift bar just off the street. It was a little outdoor restaurant he loved, with tables that led all the way up into the sand and stopped just as the beach chairs began. He could tell Nicole liked it by the way her face lit up when she realized where they were going.

"This place is great," she said, "Are we stopping for a beer?"

"It's one of my favorites," he told her, "It may have been one of your father's as well. It's been here forever, though the name has changed a few dozen times as different families run it."

"I would bet Dad liked it," she responded, "Look at that amazing view of the water." The sky was painted with a beautiful mixture of colors. And as the sun crept closer to the ocean, it sparkled as if a layer of diamonds had settled on top of the water. The people on the beach were black silhouettes as they lounged after a day in the sun.

He sat down on a barstool and, without another thought, decided this could be the perfect place for a first kiss. He lightly pulled her body between his legs and put his hands on her hips. She freely leaned her body in, dangerously close, and his heart practically leapt from his chest. "What are we doing?" she questioned, but he knew she was asking herself more than him.

"Doing something I've wanted to since the second I saw you," was all he could say before he leaned his head in the final few inches and took her mouth in his.

He was too far gone to test the waters with a soft kiss. So he grabbed the back of her neck and parted her lips to explore her mouth. Her eagerness met his as her arms came around him to deepen the kiss. He could feel the weight of her body on him, her breasts pressed hard against his chest. Neither of them could seem to get enough. Right there in a sleepy little bar on the beach, they were exploring each other with an intensity that could easily grow out of control. With that realization, he forced himself to slow his pace. He savored one last sweet taste and leaned back to look at her.

"Wow," she said, breathless.

"Wow, as in…as good as the quesadillas?" he raised his eyebrow and smirked.

"Hmm, that's quite a toss-up," she joked before adding, "It was far better than I had imagined."

"I'm glad you were imagining me, love. You had better have a seat or we may be skipping dinner all together." She laughed as she stepped away and sat down next to him. The bartender, who had seemed to be giving them a bit of privacy, came over to offer them some drinks.

Stopping for a quick shot or beer and quickly moving on was one of his favorite ways to spend time. They each took their shot of tequila and swung back some beer. "Tell me something about your father," he said to Nicole as she looked out over the ocean.

"He was amazing. I'm sure taking care of a daughter all by himself must have been hard, but I never heard him complain. He put his career goals on hold until I was old enough and he could travel again."

"What did he do?"

"He ended up practically running a company that did the computer systems for hotels and resorts."

Derek was taken a bit by surprise. He never worked closely with that part of the business, but it was still the same industry. He knew enough to be dangerous when it came to the computer systems in the hotels. He could run reports and luckily there were only a few major companies that seemed to have a majority of the business worldwide. What if her father had worked for one of them? What if he had been visiting one of Derek's properties and their paths had crossed? So many scenarios flooded his head. Trying to seem casual, he asked, "What company did he work for?"

"POS International," she replied. He knew exactly who they were, but he wasn't sure how to tell her that just yet. He was trying to stay present in the conversation and think over the past decade of people he may have met. He was pretty good with names. Bill James, though, wasn't ringing any bells at the moment.

Luckily, Nicole went on, "He oversaw the installation and training departments for the entire company. Once I was out of college, he felt comfortable traveling and shot right to the top of his company. He spent most of his time traveling around to different resorts and doing quality control visits. He was really smart, though you couldn't always tell by looking at him. He'd show up to meetings in jeans and a t-shirt and no one would take him seriously. They soon learned to though."

She was proud of him. He could see it in her eyes. He remembered from their first conversation that she was a writer for a magazine, but not much more than that. What was the name of the magazine again? "Tell me more about what you write," he suggested. Normally he asked few questions about what a woman did so that it didn't lead more into his work. He had the means to spoil each and every woman on the beach in Puerto Vallarta, yet he had always been too guarded to do that. He kept his success hidden. He had created so much for himself, but had never really been able to share it with someone. His company owned a private jet and his only travel companion so far was Gael.

"Oh, *Chicago Home Magazine*?" Nicole said, rather unenthusiastically, "I write for a column about weddings, the who's who of Chicago mostly."

"You don't like it?"

"I love weddings honestly, that part is great. Weddings, planning especially, can be hectic and horrible. I get to write about the beautiful result of all that suffering. It's the magazine itself I'm getting sick of. My boss is kind of a jerk and I'm over it. But bills gotta get paid, right?" She winked at him and took another drink of her beer.

He couldn't believe how much he wanted to tell her that she didn't have to worry about paying another bill for her entire life. Trying to take his mind off of that thought, he looked at his watch and asked, "Shall we go to dinner?"

"Yes, I'm so excited to try this restaurant," she responded, "I'm in Mexico, but my father swore this was the best Italian food he had ever had."

"He wasn't wrong. You're going to love it."

CHAPTER FIVE

Nicole loved the look of the restaurant. It was right on the Malecon and as they approached, she saw numerous couples waiting outside. She was starving, but figured it would be worth the wait. Keeping her hand in his, Derek greeted the little hostess and kissed her cheek. Her face brightened and Nicole realized she would need to get used to that happening while they were together in Mexico. Derek was so handsome; any woman would be excited to get attention from him.

Though there seemed to be quite a wait, the hostess walked them upstairs to a table with a perfect view. Nicole stopped and absorbed the ambiance of the little place. She could see why her dad had loved it. The walls were white with green vines woven all along the wooden rails on the staircase and the walls. There was a tiny bar in the back that seemed to be used by the servers more than guests. It looked as if the ivy crept around the bar as well.

The sun had completely set and the lights along the Malecon were shining brightly. There were people everywhere. Sitting up on her perch, she watched couples walking by hand in hand. There were families with children and groups of teenagers all taking in the night life. The teenagers looked like locals and Nicole wondered if they had any idea that they lived in such a gorgeous city. She wasn't naive enough to think they lived as the tourists did. She knew that their homes were far from the luxury of the hotels. But there was still that gorgeous view they got to see every day. That didn't cost a thing.

She brought her attention back to the restaurant and noticed Derek had been watching her with a smile on his face. Again, the same question went through her mind. What was she doing? She knew her situation with Andrew was rather unknown at the moment. Still, she had never done anything like this before. And Derek seemed too good to be true. There was a comfort level she felt with him in three days that she had not reached with Andrew in three years. Was it the excitement of a vacation romance? She had meant to start reading those relationship books, but just hasn't been able to crack one open yet.

"Can I order us some wine?" he asked.

"A glass of red would be great." She opened the menu and began searching for what she would like to eat.

Nicole knew a bit about wine from her waitressing days and was taken aback when Derek asked for a bottle of Chateau Lafite Rothschild. She wasn't up on all the vintages, but she knew certain years could run over a thousand dollars. She figured there was no way he was ordering one of those and went back to focusing on the menu. She remembered her father saying that he could never figure out how they could make something as simple as a Caprese salad so amazing. It only had four ingredients: fresh mozzarella, tomatoes, balsamic vinegar and basil, yet they had somehow perfected the proportions. Her heart melted when she saw it on the menu.

Just as she was about to tell this to Derek, a man walked up to the table. It turned out he was one of the owners. As Derek said his hellos, Nicole wondered how often he visited Vallarta; he seemed to know quite a few people. Before she could think too hard on the issue, she was surprised to hear Derek say, "You know your regulars quite well. This here is Bill James' daughter."

The man's face lit up and he grabbed Nicole's hands to lift her up from the chair. He took her into a full-body hug and commented on how beautiful she was. He sprinkled in a few more things in Spanish that she didn't understand, but ended with, "How is your father?"

How to answer that question? Tears came to her eyes as she took a deep breath. Derek didn't even know the specifics yet. Since the funeral, she hadn't talked out loud about the situation and honestly, she didn't want to ruin the experience of the night. She wanted this to be a celebration of his life.

"He was in a car accident. I'm here to celebrate his life and this was his favorite restaurant. We'd love to start with the Caprese salad. It was his favorite," she said it quickly and hoped that it didn't lead to a full conversation.

"*Mi amor*! I am so sorry. Yes, of course we will celebrate your father tonight. Anything you want, you get," he kissed her cheeks and held out her chair. Nicole was thankful that the wine had just arrived and that Derek had such a sweet look on his face. How could someone look like they want to kick someone's ass and make love to you all at the same moment? Derek approved the wine and they were each poured a glass.

"To your father," Derek raised his glass. Once again he knew not to push the subject. She had a feeling that when she needed to break down and deal with reality, he would be there to comfort her. But this was not that night. She raised her glass and took a drink. She could not imagine a better way to start this experience. The wine was the best she ever had. Maybe it was one of those thousand dollar bottles. At least it tasted like it could be.

"Nicole, thank you for letting me experience this with you," Derek said sincerely, "We'll talk about it more later. For now, let's enjoy the night."

She loved that idea. That was fine with her; it was a night to remember the good times. They talked mainly about her life this time. She told funny stories and he asked so many questions. He seemed to truly be interested in hearing all about her childhood with her father. It really felt like a couple out on a date night. He would occasionally reach his hand across the table to hold hers. She loved how rough they were, a feeling that could only have come from being a fighter.

At one point, Derek took a work call. Since he didn't excuse himself from the table, Nicole could tell that it must be pretty important in his company. He sounded like a boss talking to a subordinate- not rude, but giving directions and making decisions. She liked that he had both brawn and brains. He had to send a few text messages as well, but took care that she didn't feel ignored. He checked the messages quickly, replied, and immediately put his phone away.

The evening was perfect. The food was delicious; she could see why her father had loved it so much. She promised the owner to come back before she left. As they walked back out onto the Malecon, a little black car drove up. Derek led them to it. Nicole was surprised to see Hector driving. He hopped out of the car with as much enthusiasm as he had when he showed her to her room. He held the door open for her as she got into the backseat. As Derek slid in next to her, she whispered, "What is going on? Why is Hector picking us up?"

"He's become my driver while I'm here. I get to places quickly and he gets some extra cash," he winked and wrapped his arm around her, "Should we have a drink at the bar?"

She couldn't believe the words that came out of her mouth, "Let's grab a bottle in the market next door and go up to my room. I have a balcony."

"You heard the boss, Hector. Drop us off at the market, please."

"Yes, of course, *señor*."

Within minutes, they were back to the Romantic Zone and pulling up to the market next to her hotel. They wandered through the small aisles and again Derek kept her hand in his. There was a protectiveness about him that she loved. Feeling such strength so close to her was quite the turn on. She couldn't believe that she wasn't nervous. She was by no means a virgin, but she had met Derek two days ago. And she had every intention of sleeping with him tonight. Dinner was about her father, tonight was about them. Tomorrow, she would think about everything else. Perhaps after spending the night with Derek she would know what to do about Andrew. So for now, she pushed Andrew out of her head.

Derek stopped by the hotel bar and got two wine glasses and a wine key from the bartender. While they were on the short ride in the elevator, Nicole could barely look in his direction. Now it was hitting her. She stared at her feet and prayed for the doors to open. Next thing she knew, she was leading him through the door of her room. Nicole walked into the bathroom to check out how she looked. She stared back at her reflection- a little black halter-top sun dress showing off her bare shoulders, blond hair long down her back, her face and shoulders tanned from the past two days. She gave herself a reassuring look. She was doing the right thing. Nicole could hear Derek opening the wine as she walked back into the room. It was a basic room, but there was space for a king bed and loveseat and a nice view of the water.

He handed her a glass of wine and had one poured for himself.

"Should we sit outside, love?"

"Have I told you how much I love that you have a little pet name for me?" She took the glass and headed toward the balcony.

"No, you haven't. I'm glad you like it. It suits you." He hadn't realized he had given her a nickname. He always did like how everyone in Mexico referred to women as *"mi amor"*. It must have rubbed off on him. He leaned against the balcony and watched her as she sat down. "Are you thinking about your Maybe Boyfriend back home?" he asked.

"I'm trying not to. I'm focusing on you tonight." She set her wine glass down on the table and walked over to him. "This doesn't feel wrong. That has to mean something, right?" she asked him, not really expecting an answer. "I want this to be about us, not him. I'll worry about him tomorrow."

He wrapped his hand behind her neck and as he pulled her to him, he whispered, "I want it to always be about us. You never have to worry again."

This time when he kissed her there wasn't the desperation they felt the first time. They had all night to linger and discover each other. Nicole felt like she was in a fantasy. It didn't feel real; he didn't feel real. She couldn't wrap her head around how he felt about her. The things he said, could he really mean them? She was surprised how much, in this moment, she wanted them to be true.

Sex with Andrew was good. Not great, but good. Sometimes, when she wasn't feeling inspired, she would imagine them in a different situation. She didn't fantasize about other men, just that they were living a different life. This wasn't going to be an issue tonight. She was living the fantasy. There's no way her imagination could come up with something more exciting than this.

Derek's kiss was slow but strong. His tongue searched all over her mouth. He kissed her lips, her chin, her neck, all as if he was trying to absorb as much of her as he could. He took her face in his hands and looked into her eyes.

"Let me take you inside," he whispered.

Nicole could barely speak. She nodded her head and the next thing she knew, he reached his hands down to the backs of her thighs and picked her up off the ground. She instinctively wrapped her legs around his waist and he carried her back into her hotel room. Derek supported her back as he laid them both down onto the bed. He was looking down at her and his breathing had quickened.

"What are you doing to me?" he asked her and this time he waited for an answer.

"I can't explain this," was all that she could think to say. It seemed to satisfy his curiosity because he lowered himself on to top of her and took her mouth in his again. And her fantasy continued. The night before, she had been in this very bed, imagining what it would be like to have Derek there with her. Now here he was, his weight on top of her exhilarating.

He took his time kissing her. Nicole wasn't hugely into foreplay, but she enjoyed that he didn't seem rushed to get to sex. She grasped the back of his shirt and lifted it up enough to feel the strong muscles along his back. A raspy moan came from his mouth and he began kissing lower on her neck. The style of dress didn't give him full access to her breasts, so he slowly inched it from her thighs to her waist and over her chest. She lifted her arms for him. He pulled it off of her and tossed it across the room. Then he reached under her and unhooked her little black bra. That sailed through the air as well. Then she pulled his shirt off and there they were, him in linen pants and her in her little black thong.

She could see more tattoos and her heart skipped a beat again. He had some hair scattered across his chest. Even though it had a tint of grey to it, it was still extremely sexy. His chest was tanned from his trip and very muscular. He had big tattoos covering both shoulders, one on his chest, and a few that trailed down his biceps. She wanted to know what each one meant to him. Her tattoos were all meaningful to her and she wanted to know the stories behind his.

He leaned back over her, but this time began kissing the side of her breasts. He took her hands and held them both over her head and sweetly kissed the tip of her nipple. Then he put it in his mouth and it instantly hardened against him. His mouth was so warm. She pushed her head back into the pillow, taking in the sensation.

His head came back up and found her mouth again. She loved kissing him. She could feel that he was ready. She freed her hands from his and searched for his pants, working quickly on his button and zipper and pulling them down over his hips. She had long enough legs to hook a foot on the waist of his pants and boxers and push them the rest of the way down to his feet. He lifted his head and smiled at her little trick. Now that they were eye to eye, he began kissing her again, whispering sweet things to her between kisses. He talked about how beautiful she was, that she hadn't left his mind since the moment he saw her.

He slipped off her underwear, lingering slowly down her legs as he pulled them off. When he came back to kiss her again, he was completely on top of her. She wrapped her legs around his back, ready to take him all in. He thrust slowly inside of her and kept the rhythm at a passionate pace. She grabbed onto each of his biceps and her mind went completely blank. She had never felt this much chemistry with someone, especially the first time.

He knew exactly what to do to please her. When he increased the speed, it didn't take long to take her over the edge. Every muscle in her body contracted and released and she felt pleasure over her entire body as she reached orgasm. Just as it began to subside, he knew what to do in order to make it happen again. Over and over, he pushed her body to the limit. Finally, he pulled out, making sure not to cum inside of her. She was glad to be on birth control, realizing just then that they hadn't even talked about it.

Derek reached for the shirt he had been wearing and quickly cleaned them both up. He laid back down and cradled her head in the crook of his arm. They rested quietly for a few minutes, enjoying the moment. He traced his finger up and down her body and she stretched her fingers in the hair on his chest. She felt more peaceful than she ever had before. All in an instant she didn't want to think about leaving him in two weeks. She closed her eyes and hoped that, for now, he would stay the night.

CHAPTER SIX

When he woke up, Derek realized that he and Nicole had barely moved the entire night. She was still curled up with her head resting on his shoulder. Her leg had crept higher up on top of him and his hand was holding her thigh. It was early. He craned his neck to see the watch on the wrist that was underneath Nicole- 6:30am. He had a breakfast meeting with Gael, who had flown to Chicago the day before. He knew from the call last night that the trip had gone well and he was looking forward to hearing about the details.

He looked down at Nicole's body sprawled over him. He couldn't imagine her not being there every morning. Having a connection to Chicago was important to him now. He wouldn't push through this deal unless it was perfect for all involved, but he realized he was considering buying a place there if it didn't. This would be the first time he'd have a residence in the States since he was twenty-five. Nicole was worth it.

She stirred when Derek slid himself from the bed.

"Good morning," she yawned to him as he wandered into the bathroom.

"Good morning, love," he called back to her from the bathroom.

"Are you leaving?" she asked in the cutest voice he had ever heard.

He realized he was at a crossroads with himself. He had never told a woman about his company. Silvia didn't even know the extent of it. She just thought he had ownership in some hotels in Puerto and Nuevo

Vallarta. She didn't know about his international business. Derek knew he didn't want to lie to Nicole, but wasn't sure he was ready to open up about this either. He decided the best thing to do was to explain who Gael was without going into detail about his business.

"I have a meeting this morning. The man on the phone last night is here as well and we need to meet for breakfast." That was honest, he thought.

"Oh, I assumed you were on vacation. Are you here for work?" She wasn't dumb, that he had already figured out. He knew he had to give her more and he was okay with that.

He walked back into the room and sat next to her on the bed. "I am originally from Detroit. But, my company does business in different areas. A few are here. I spend time in all of the locations and have been here for the past few months." That would do. Trying to keep it light, he added, "You don't think a guy from Detroit could have a tan like this if he hadn't been here awhile, did you?" He winked, leaning over to kiss her.

"Must be nice," she laughed. Then she flung her arms around him and pulled him back into bed. "Do you really have to go?" she asked and kissed him deeply. Somehow she didn't sound desperate. He figured maybe it was because he'd ask her the same question if it were her getting ready to leave.

"I do. Would you like to meet me on the Malecon afterwards?"

"Sure, I'll go for a run first," she said, "And I need to call my best friend and tell her where I am." She looked nervous. He wondered if she was thinking about the Maybe Boyfriend as well. He'd love to get him on the phone and tell him about his amazing time with Nicole last night. His blood began to boil just thinking about this other guy. This was going to need to get figured out soon. He knew he had a protective side, but this was hovering dangerously close to insane jealously.

He kissed her one more time and pulled himself from the bed. "I've gotta stop by my place and change clothes. Good thing it's acceptable to walk around shirtless here." He wouldn't be putting his shirt back on after last night. Nicole laughed as she remembered Derek using it to clean them both.

"Where are you staying?" she asked.

Without even thinking he answered, "The Paraíso, next door." In the past, he avoided the question or had even lied about where he stayed. He knew he didn't want to take that route with Nicole; there wasn't any harm in her knowing.

"Oh good, you don't have to go far shirtless. I don't want you making too many women faint from those pecs," she teased. God, he loved her personality. Not only was she gorgeous and great in bed, she was smart, interesting, and funny. This woman was the entire package. Once the Maybe Boyfriend was taken care of, at least.

"They'll survive," he said as he put his pants on, "Meet me at 11:00am at the beach bar from yesterday. And, wear a bathing suit." and he headed for the door.

He closed the door behind him and headed for the staircase. As he came back into the lobby, he could see that the office door was open. He made eye contact with Silvia. "Shit," he whispered. She looked pissed. Of course the fact that he was shirtless wasn't going to help the situation. He hoped she'd stay in the office and fester about it rather than come out and make a scene in front of the entire hotel. But she stood up, so he cracked his neck and braced for the latter.

Silvia was small but she was tough. He had seen her temper on occasion. She stormed over to him and hit his arm. "What do you think you're doing?"

"Silvia, this isn't the place."

"I don't care, *pendejo*!" He lifted an eyebrow at her, knowing she had just called him an asshole. "It was that blond bitch, wasn't it? I heard you two hung out for hours the other day, even after I left. Didn't waste any time, did you?"

He realized this was going to be a mess. He couldn't care less what she said to him. But was she stupid enough to say something to Nicole? She was still a paying customer. He hadn't thought to tell Nicole about Silvia and now he wished he had. What would Nicole think if Silvia found her before he had a chance to explain? He contemplated going back up to the room immediately, then figured he'd try to talk to Silvia first.

"We aren't together anymore," he told her, "I'm not doing anything wrong."

"I know about your little rule, you *idiota*," she yelled.

"Well, I broke it," was all he could think to say. He didn't have time for this shit. He needed to get changed to meet Gael, so he took his phone out of his pocket and called the general manager. He could hear Silvia going on in a mixture of English and Spanish, but did his best to tune her out.

"Hi, Victor, it's Derek…There is a guest here. I want to make sure that Silvia has absolutely no contact with her. Her job depends on it. Yes, she's the one…yes, I know you told me this would happen…*gracias*."

He shoved the phone back in his pocket. He looked down at Silvia, trying to show her that he was not kidding. "You leave her alone. You do not speak to her. Your job depends on it," he repeated. He waited for a response, but she just turned around, stomped back into the office, and slammed the door like a child throwing a fit.

Derek looked around and the girls behind the counter were trying to pretend like they hadn't seen the whole thing. Derek glanced at the rest of the lobby; luckily it was too early for any guests to be at the bar or tables. Maybe if guests had been around, she wouldn't have caused such a scene. He'd have to remember to stay later from now on. That made him smile, in spite of everything that just went down. Victor had warned him that this would happen if he ever hooked up with a guest and Silvia found out about it. He rubbed his head as he headed out to the street. He hated the idea of causing any problems for Victor. He should have never gone out with an employee.

He walked into his apartment and started the shower before wandering back into the bedroom, stripping off his remaining clothes. He laid back on the bed with his feet still touching the floor. He stayed there for a few minutes, naked, thinking about everything.

First he tried with Silvia and now he was enamored with Nicole. Was he really tired of living this life? Maybe he was looking for a little bit of normalcy and thought having a girlfriend would help make that happen. So were his feelings for Nicole genuine? Or did they come on so quickly because of this new need to be with someone? That question scared the shit out of him. He needed to figure it out quickly. He didn't want to hurt her.

"Fuck!" he yelled out to the empty apartment. He stood up, wondering if he should go back up to explain everything to Nicole. Gael could wait. He stood in the shower, letting the hot water hit his face and run down his body as the bathroom filled with steam. Last night was perfect; he didn't want to taint it so soon. Luckily, he had already explained to her that he had been in Vallarta for a few months. This potential problem wouldn't come quite so out of left field now.

What would they do for the rest of her trip? They wouldn't be able to avoid Silvia. He wasn't even going to try. But he didn't want their time together to be marred by Silvia either though. He couldn't believe that the idea of them staying at the Paraíso even entered his head, yet it did. However, with his new worry about the root of his intense feelings for Nicole, he didn't think that was a good idea. Sure, he was already planning trips to Chicago in his head. But they had only spent two days together. He couldn't get ahead of himself. He couldn't believe how many times he had said that to himself since he met Nicole. He had protected his personal life this long and wasn't prepared to share that with her yet. But she was here for two weeks and every day got closer to her getting on a plane back to Chicago.

He turned off the water and wrapped a towel around his waist. He quickly grabbed some board shorts and a t-shirt. He didn't need to worry about what Gael thought. He was only thinking of his time with Nicole on the beach. He threw on sunglasses and flip-flops and grabbed his wallet and phone, stowing them in his pockets on his way out the door.

CHAPTER SEVEN

Nicole stayed in bed for a while after Derek left, thinking about the night before. Even in her wildest fantasies, she had never experienced anything as sensual as making love to Derek Stone. She could still smell him in the room and on her skin, could still feel his hands all over her. Even when he wasn't with her, he was still haunting her. She remembered his eyes, such a dark brown that the iris almost flowed right into the pupils, an amazing combination of kindness and mystery.

There was some serious depth behind those eyes. She couldn't put her finger on it. She wasn't worried about baggage, but she felt there was a story there. Maybe it was the writer in her. Through the years, she had interviewed hundreds of people for her column and she had learned that some people were very two-dimensional- what you see is what you get. It wasn't that they were boring or bad people, there just wasn't much to dig up. Derek, on the other hand, his eyes were like deep pools filled with so much to uncover, layers of stories to discover what had turned him into the man who made love to her. There was a connection between them that she couldn't deny. She couldn't wait to get him back in bed, a feeling she hadn't had about Andrew maybe ever.

She knew she wanted to think about Andrew on her run, so she turned her thoughts to her best friend Kate. She had been in Mexico for three nights now and hadn't even turned on her phone. She just couldn't do it before. She needed some time away from it all. Depending on how concerned or angry Andrew was, he may have called Kate to see if she knew anything. A dilemma presented itself. Should she keep her phone off and give her friend plausible deniability? No, Kate would go crazy with worry. She may have already. *What the hell*, she thought.

Nicole leaned over the bed and reached for her purse, practically falling to the ground before snatching it at the last second. She pulled out her phone and turned it on, closing her eyes as she waited to see how many voicemails she had. When she finally heard the dings, she looked at her screen- seven voicemails and ten text messages. Not as bad as she had expected. She looked at the text messages first. There was one from her boss and one from a coworker, both sending her well wishes. She also had two more from friends checking on how she was doing.

The final six were from Kate, sounding more concerned as the messages went on. She thought Nicole was just ignoring her. The last one simply read "Call me PLEASE!!" Even though Nicole had the voicemails to listen to, it didn't appear that Andrew had called Kate. She had complicated feelings about that. She wasn't too upset. Really, it was somewhat of a relief. But she was irritated that Andrew didn't seem concerned about her.

Nicole clicked her voicemail button and waited to hear the first one. It was Kate, of course. She was rather calm as she said, "Hi, sweetie! Thinking about you, call me when you want to talk." Then the second message, "Nic, checking again, love you." By the third message, she was beginning to sound concerned, "Nicole, is everything okay? I'm getting worried about you. Please call me." At the fourth, Nicole could tell that she was trying not to sound mad, "I know you're going through a lot right now, please call me. I'm ready to call Andrew." *Oh no, that isn't good*, Nicole thought. The fifth was a random call from a colleague about covering one of her weddings. The sixth was Kate again, "Andrew didn't answer his phone either. What is going on? I may start stalking you and come by your place." Nicole laughed after hearing that. It had only been three days and she was ready to send out a search party.

The seventh message was from Andrew. All he said was, "I'm dodging calls from Kate. Are you ready to tell me where you are?" He had no idea where she was. Apparently he hadn't been listening to all those stories she had told him about her father. At least he hadn't talked to Kate yet. Well, as of early this morning he hadn't.

She rolled her eyes and called Kate. There was barely time for a ring on her end when…

"NICOLE! What is going on? Why haven't you returned my calls?"

"Hey, babe," Nicole practically started crying with happiness just being on the phone with her. Where to start? She needed to tell her best friend everything. Kate may not always agree with every decision she made, but she always listened and supported her. "Guess where I am?"

"What? Guess? My mind has been going nuts trying to figure that out." Though Kate started to sound relieved, there was still tension in her voice.

"After the funeral, I booked a ticket to Vallarta," Nicole said.

"Ticket? Singular? Is Andrew with you?"

"Nope, didn't want to come."

"Are you fucking kidding me? Why didn't you call me? You know I would have gone," Kate was practically yelling.

"I know," she soothed, "I didn't care that I would be alone. I just wanted to get here."

Kate began to lecture when Nicole cut her off. "Kate, I met someone."

Silence.

"Start talking," was all Kate had to say. Nicole spilled the entire story, ending with Derek leaving her room that morning.

Silence again.

Nicole waited and let her process everything. It wasn't long before Kate decided to speak, "You know I love Andrew, right? But it sounds like from what you've said, this guy, or someone like him, is far more suited for you. Maybe your dad sent you there to find your true love."

Wow, Nicole thought. That was out of character for Kate. She was usually far too practical to use the term "true love". She knew that Kate didn't believe in soul mates and true love came pretty close. Kate continued, "Most girls would be screaming for a ring after three years and marriage hasn't even been on your radar. But you sound crazy about this guy. Is this a vacation fling?"

"Kate, I can't imagine waking up another day without him there. I've known him for three days; I think I'm losing it." She hung her arm over her eyes to block out the world. She did feel like she was going crazy and it felt good to say it out loud.

"Who knows, Nicole, maybe this is where the term 'crazy about someone' was coined. It's ridiculously early, but it does sound very intense between you two." She had a good point. But was "crazy about someone" the same as really being in love with them? Nicole needed to think. She needed to run.

"I need to figure out what's going on with me, with Andrew, with Derek," she said, "Please don't say anything to Andrew if he calls you. I just need some time to decide what I'm going to do."

Kate agreed. They finished talking and Nicole promised not to go another day without calling her. They said their goodbyes and Nicole got out of bed.

It was only 8:30 and already hot out. Still, she hoped to get a few miles in before the sun began to singe her skin. She headed out to the beach and began at a slow jog.

Nicole loved to run. It let her concentrate on one thing and block out the rest of the world. She would let her head spin with thoughts and memories. Everything swirled around and her mind grasped onto the things that were really important. As she ran, she realized that she was analyzing her relationship with Andrew. It was mild natured and peaceful. But as she remembered back over the last three years, she noticed that everything stayed within Andrew's comfort zone, which meant that Nicole had abandoned the parts of herself that would disrupt the vibe of their relationship. She wasn't sure whose fault that was. Snapping back into reality, she realized her hands were clenched and she was almost at a full sprint.

She slowed herself to a stop, relaxing her hands and leaning over to take in a few deep breaths. So part of her was content and comfortable with Andrew, but not the whole part. How important was that? Can couples really love all of each other? Should she have stirred the pot a few times, made him uncomfortable to make herself happy? She couldn't deny that they had been happy together. They had fun times and she had enjoyed his company. She wouldn't have stayed with him if that hadn't been true.

She set back into a jog as she thought about all of those good times. Then she tried to think about the bad. They didn't really fight, but was that necessarily a good thing? She wished she had started reading those relationship books…

Derek flashed into her mind and she wondered if they would fight. For some reason, she thought that they might. Not all the time, of course, but imagine the amazing make-up sex when they did. Given the level of comfort she already felt with him, it seemed like they'd each feel safe enough to give their opinions on things regardless if the other agreed. *Isn't that how most fights start anyway?* she wondered.

She needed to stay focused on Andrew. Nicole still wasn't completely sure what to think of the fight they had when she was packing. Even if Derek wasn't in the picture, would she still be mad enough to break it off? That may be the question that would answer everything.

She forced herself to stay calm while running; she didn't want to overheat. She decided it was a good time to turn around and make this the halfway point of her run. It had been half an hour so she had gone maybe two miles? It was harder to run in the sand so, even with the sprint, she knew her pace had to be slower.

She knew she wasn't mad that Andrew didn't go with her. She couldn't have expected Derek to drop everything and go with her. Regardless, she was a grown woman capable of traveling on her own. It was that Andrew left the apartment as if she would be home that night to work everything out. He stayed away long enough for her to leave.

That was the kicker. That wasn't right. If people should live their lives by the old rules that you don't go to bed angry or say something you can't take back, this was pretty bad. What if the plane crashed? What if something horrible happened? He'd have no idea. He should have at least made her tell him where she was going. If he didn't care, that spoke volumes. And what she heard was that it was over with Andrew. She couldn't imagine going back to the life they led together. She needed more excitement, more passion now.

She needed Derek. Or at least someone like Derek. She tried to remind herself again that she had only known him for three days. It was way too early to know if he was "the one." Nicole thought back to her previous boyfriends before Andrew, the guys that were more like Derek. How did their relationships feel in the beginning?

Nick had been funny and they laughed a lot. Mike was exciting and kept her on her toes (as it turned out, he had kept a lot of other girls on their toes as well). Jason was sexy and mysterious, but moody. None of them seemed to have all of the characteristics she was looking for. And none of them were successful like Andrew. She had given up that excitement for a type of dependability. She never wanted Andrew for his money, but she had liked that he was stable. All of the bad boys had broken her heart and she had had a nice guy in Andrew. Derek seemed to have all of these qualities rolled into one sexy package. But still, none of her relationships had seemed as intense this early on.

Had Kate been right? Did her dad send her to Vallarta to meet Derek? Was that even possible? She liked the idea. She knew her dad would have loved spending time with Derek over Andrew any day. He hadn't spent lots of time with Andrew. Her father loved Andrew for loving her, but she could always tell that he didn't quite see what the appeal was. They were very different from each other. Her father never showed his success in how he dressed or carried himself. He liked it better that way. It seemed blaringly obvious right now that maybe Derek could have been sent to her so she would see what she was missing. Maybe he wouldn't end up being the one. But he had shown her that Andrew wasn't either. Andrew was a good person and he would be perfect for someone else. Could her dad have known that? Did he now have the power to show her through Derek?

Thinking about her father made her sad again. She was finally here in Puerto Vallarta and yet she hadn't spent a lot of time focusing on him. She had initially imagined this trip as a time to soul search by herself in a place where she could feel closer to her dad. She hadn't even found the King's Head Pub yet. She decided to make a list of places to go when she got back to the hotel room. She'd have plenty of time before she needed to meet Derek.

Nicole made her way up the beach to the hotel entrance, stopping by the bar just at the edge of the beach for a bottle of water. She caught her breath and cooled her body and began to head toward the elevator. She could see two female employees out of the corner of her eye. It looked like they were talking about her. One was a short little thing and she was giving Nicole the stink eye as she spoke to the other woman. Nicole wondered if she really looked that out of shape from her run. Just as she shrugged them off, Hector walked up to her and hurried her over to the elevator. *"Mi buena,* how was your run?" He was too cute for words.

"Hi, Hector. It was hot. How are you?"

"Always good. When you are ready to meet *Señor* Derek, you come straight to me and I'll take you there." Wow, she could get kind of used to a driver.

"Thanks, I'll be down in about an hour." She pushed the elevator door. Hector stood there waiting with her. She glanced around and the lobby seemed slow enough. Maybe he wasn't needed up at the front. She tried to think of small talk. "Are you going upstairs as well?"

"Oh yes, I have to see to the maids' supplies on your floor," he said with a big, bright smile.

As the elevator arrived and climbed to the second floor, Nicole again tried to fill the silence. "You will be able to leave while you are working? You won't get in trouble for that?" She was concerned for Hector. He was such a nice man; she didn't want him getting in any trouble over her. She could easily catch a cab or, if she hurried, she could walk it.

"No, *señorita,* I can do any driving for Senor Derek. No trouble at all." He stepped off the elevator as it opened.

As she reached her door, she told Hector that she would see him soon. Nicole wondered how Derek was able to get the hotel to allow Hector to leave whenever he needed a ride. She stepped into her air-conditioned room and practically shivered. She wanted to shower first and then she'd figure out a schedule to make sure she visited each and every place on her list of her father's favorite places.

CHAPTER EIGHT

Derek was impressed with how well Gael did on his first solo trip. He knew he was a bit of a control freak when it came to business. For his entire life, he had to do everything for himself. That was what he was used to. Stepping back and letting Gael take the lead on this meeting was huge for him. Most of the business side would ultimately be done by the hotel company. Derek's company was there for their expertise in finding lucrative locations. Gael had gone above and beyond. Not only had he been thorough in his review and on-site visit of the location, he had already found a contact within the Chicago city government to get the paperwork started for necessary permits for their clients. He had been meticulous in his groundwork. The hotel developer's return on investment would be nice, which translated to money for Derek. All that was needed was for Derek and the client to give their seals of approval.

Derek was not willing to give up any time in Vallarta with Nicole. Still, he wasn't sure how quickly they could lose this location. Even a day trip would require over twelve hours with travel time. As he and Gael sat on the balcony of the little bar, he stirred his drink with the straw and considered his options. Gael was quite confident in his impression of the location and Gael was a smart man. He was very cautious with situations and didn't trust anything easily. Derek knew he had worked quietly in his past with a federal investigative agency in Mexico. He obviously didn't know details, but he knew Gael could be dead serious when needed. He had proven his abilities over the years and Derek trusted his opinion.

"Here's what I'm thinking," he raised his eyes from his drink, "This should be your baby. I still want my living quarters, but if you take the lead on this and it goes through, half the finder's fee and the percentage of revenue will go directly to you." Gael's face lit with excitement. He was usually rather serious; Derek enjoyed seeing this lighter side.

"Let's do a shot." It was a tradition for them after coming to a business decision. Gael waved over the server and asked for two shots of tequila chilled and dressed.

Derek could tell he was struggling a bit to keep his composure. This could be quite a chunk of change for Gael. "This will be on top of your regular salary and bonuses," he added.

"I will drink to that, *amigo*," Gael laughed and they both threw back their glasses of tequila.

Glancing at his watch, Derek could see that it was nearing 11am. He had asked Hector to keep his eye on Nicole as best he could and to drive her to the bar on the beach. His run-in with Silvia had been right at the edge of his thoughts all morning. "I have somewhere I need to be," he told Gael, "Let's talk later." He threw enough money on the table to cover the bill and a sizeable tip.

"Have fun with your lady," Gael teased.

"She's something," he told him as he put on his sunglasses.

The bar was a short walk away and Derek enjoyed the little bit of exercise. He hadn't gone for a run yet today and his legs were itching to move. He was pleased with his decision with Gael, who deserved the chance to prove himself. During the past ten years, he hadn't had a hectic forty-hour work week in the concrete jungle, but he did ultimately shoulder all of the responsibility in his company. It would be nice to have Gael take on more of partnership role, to have someone that could allow Derek to take weeks at a time off to disappear to some corner of the globe, to be unreachable. He knew this wasn't to be taken lightly. This would be a serious decision, but he liked where they were headed.

He felt like he just may be ready to share his personal life with someone else now. He could imagine sharing this world he had created with Nicole. He always knew his lifestyle would be hard for someone else. Most people would not want to live away from their family. Nicole didn't have any family left. Both of her parents were only children and they were gone now. She didn't have grandparents, aunts, uncles, or cousins. She was very much in the same situation he was. She was in this world rather alone. Her situation fit well into his lifestyle.

With that thought still floating in his mind, he saw her sitting at the bar. He liked that she had already ordered herself a drink. It wasn't a beer this time, but some sort of mixed drink with an umbrella in it. She was wearing the black bathing suit from the day he met her. This time she had on a pair of cute little board shorts and a white tank top with material so thin, it looked about ready to disintegrate. She was looking out at the water, lost in her own thoughts. He could see that Hector had given her the beach bag he asked for.

He walked up to her and kissed the top of her head as he slid into the seat next to her. "Hope I didn't keep you waiting."

"Hi." She leaned over and gave him a quick kiss on the lips, as if she had been doing it her whole life. "I brought Hector's mystery bag." She smiled and lifted the huge bag off the ground for a second.

"No mystery, just some beach necessities. Towels, sun screen for that gorgeous skin, some chips and pico de gallo to snack on. I figured we could get water and drinks from the bar."

"Hector is too funny. He wouldn't tell me what was inside. Just said '*Señor* Derek' required some things." Her imitation of Hector was hilarious and spot on. "I wasn't sure if I should add mule to my resume or expect whips and chains."

"No, love, I never got into drugs with my fighting career. We can indulge in the occasion blindfolding, but I'm not really into the S&M thing. Were you looking forward to being whipped?"

She blushed, but laughed and ordered him a beer to avoid answering. "I would have had a beer waiting for you, but didn't want it to get warm," she said.

"That's quite alright. I just appreciate that you remember what kind I drink," he responded.

They decided to go down by the water for a while and then have a leisurely lunch. He wanted to take her shopping afterwards, but he wasn't sure if she'd be receptive to the idea of him spoiling her just yet. She closed out her tab, paying for her drink and his beer. Although he would have preferred to pay for it, he understood that she was probably trying to show that she didn't expect him to always pay for things. It was a nice gesture and it just made him fall for her even harder.

They chose the two lounge chairs closest to the water that were still in the bar's territory. He took off his shirt and laid it on the back on the chair. He couldn't take his eyes off Nicole while she slipped the tiny tank top over her head and let her shorts fall to her feet. When she stepped out of them, she kicked them up into her hands. She did have nice little tricks with those legs of hers. He remembered her underneath him the night before, pushing his pants down with her foot. He couldn't wait to get on top of her again.

He pulled two small towels out of the bag, laid them on the chairs, and then handed over the sunblock, telling her, "The SPF isn't too high. You'll still get a tan, if you'd like." She put a small coat on her arms, stomach, and legs. The way her hands rubbed all over her body was incredibly sexy. He'd taken many women to the beach over the years and they always tried to entice him while they applied lotion. But for some reason when a woman was trying too hard to be sexy, it always got lost in translation for him. Nicole, however, was all business and it made her even more adorable. It almost seemed that she didn't realize how gorgeous she actually was. The Maybe Boyfriend of hers should have been telling her every day.

"Okay, let me help with your shoulders and back or I'm going to have to ravish you right here and now," he said, reaching for the bottle.

Nicole laughed out loud like he had said the most absurd thing. "Are you serious? This is turning you on?" Still giggling, she handed over the bottle. "Am I not going to be able to take you out in public?" She turned her body away from him so that he could help put it on her back. He realized rather quickly that it may have been worse than watching her. He kept his composure with her shoulders until she turned her head just a bit and looked at him from the corner of her eyes. She bit her lip slightly and smiled. He wanted to have her right there. As he rubbed his hands down her back and along the small curves of her hips, he could feel himself starting to get hard.

"We need to get into the water now," he announced and grabbed her hand. She just rolled her eyes and laughed at him and they headed toward the water at almost a run. He dove straight into a wave to cool off and get control of his body. The water was about waist-high. Nicole waded over to him and slowly put her arms around his neck. Her skin felt warm against his which compared to the cold water felt soothing. She leaned her head against his shoulder. He was 5'10" and he guessed her height at about 5'7". She fit against his body perfectly. They stayed there, still and quiet for a few minutes, enjoying the moment.

"This is nice," she practically whispered and took a deep breath. He didn't need to reply; it felt like she was saying it for the both of them. He tilted her chin up towards him and took her mouth into his. If there weren't families playing around them, he would have made love to her right there in the water. They were definitely going to have to come back to the beach at night, when they could enjoy each other in the water under the cover of dark with the moonlight shining over them.

He kissed her slow but deep, wanting to taste every part of her mouth. He couldn't imagine ever taking her kisses for granted. This would never get old. The feel of her lips and the taste of her mouth, nothing had ever felt so much like home to him. He grabbed her hair at the back on her neck and tugged slightly. She let out a moan and he kissed her along her cheek bone. He saw her take a quick glance over toward the closest family to make sure that the kids weren't watching and he forced himself to pull away from her.

They both dunked their heads under the water and watched all the tiny little fish swimming around them. There were schools of them darting everywhere. Nicole had never experienced that before and she laughed and pointed like a little girl. She was so comfortable in her skin. He loved that about her. They waded deeper into the water and let the waves crash into them and bring them back closer to shore. Derek always made sure to have a tight hold of her hand each time, so there was no risk of the ocean grabbing hold of her in the undertow.

Out in the water just a bit, where families were playing, was a floating trampoline. Kids were jumping off of it and laughing. Derek watched Nicole as she smiled at the kids. One did a front flip and she clapped and cheered for him. When she saw Derek watching her, she told him that she used to be a gymnast when she was younger.

"Wanna give it a try?" he asked.

"Definitely!" She smiled and started swimming towards it. As they reached the ropes attached to the side of the floating island, Nicole grabbed a hold and hiked herself on top of it. Derek was impressed with her abilities, but hoped that he would have been able to cop a feel while assisting her. She turned and looked down at him.

"Coming up?" she smiled, blocking the sun out of her eyes.

"On my way," he yelled up to her and pulled himself up onto the trampoline. Since the kids hadn't climbed on again, Nicole jumped and laughed and did a few flips in the air. *She really does love life*, he thought.

"Are you going to try a flip over the edge?" he asked, knowing that's what got her excited while watching.

"Wanna see me do a backflip?" she looked ready to impress him.

"Let's see it!" He walked over and kissed her cheek.

She went closer to the edge and leaned over to take a look. She turned and faced him, standing as close to the edge as she could. Then she began to hesitate. "I just realized that it might be twenty years since I've done a backflip." She had a look of terror in her eyes. "I can't believe I'm this freaked out."

"Oh love, you don't have to do it then." He started to feel bad for her.

"Yes, I do," she said quickly, maybe before she could think too much about it. She got a look of determination on her face, winked at him, and flew her body back over her head. He ran up to see as he heard a huge splash in the water. Moments after she went under, she shot back up, laughing and cheering for herself. He would have been impressed regardless, but he was extremely proud, considering she did it in spite of being scared.

He dove into the water after her and she threw her arms around him as soon as she could. She was beaming from the experience.

"I'm very proud of you!" he said between kisses.

They swam a bit closer to the shore so that they could both reach the bottom easily. He saw her shiver a bit when a gust of wind came, so he picked her up and threw her over his shoulder. She laughed and hit his butt and kicked her legs. He just squeezed tighter until he reached the beach and set her down in the sand.

"You seemed cold; I thought I'd get you to your towel," he said with a smile.

"You are crazy!" was all she could say before he wrapped her towel around her and pulled her into him to warm her with his body heat as well. They settled on their chairs under the sun. Derek couldn't take his eyes off of her, from her wet blond hair to her body glistening in the sunshine. Her tiny black bikini left little to the imagination when it was wet. It looked almost as if it were painted on her breasts. All over her body, he began to notice the tattoos she had hidden. There was one just behind her ear, one on the back of her neck. She had a date down the side of her rib cage and he wondered what the significance was. She had one on her ankle as well. He couldn't quite see what it was and she noticed him looking.

"It's a lotus flower," she told him, "The roots are in mud and they rise up out of it to bloom." She closed her eyes again to block the intense sun, but she looked like she was soaking up every ounce of it.

"That is nice," he said, "maybe that should be my next one." He liked the idea of them sharing a tattoo. He had never done that before. "Tell me about all of them."

"My first was the lotus flower. My father took me when I was sixteen years old. It can represent so many things, but ultimately for me, it was my mother. The mud represents the cancer. Now she's up in heaven, out of pain." He was impressed with her choice of tattoo at such a young age. She went on, "I didn't want an angel; it seemed too obvious. When I saw the Buddhist meaning of a lotus, I knew it was perfect."

"And this one?" he said, brushing her hair aside and touching the little swirl behind her ear.

"This one is a symbol I saw once that stands for 'strength'," she smiled, "I thought it was pretty, too."

"What does 'so it goes' mean on the back of your neck?" He reached his hand under her neck and she moaned just a tiny bit.

"It's from the book Slaughterhouse-Five. It was my favorite book in college. It roughly means that shit happens, so I better deal with it."

He liked that as well. So far they were all significant, none from a drunken night that she immediately regretted. So many people these days had ridiculous pictures stamped on their bodies, for no reason other than too many drinks and bad decisions. "What about this?" he ran his finger down her rib cage and she squirmed.

"That's my mother's birthday. I've already been thinking I should get my father's on the other side."

"Want to go get it?"

She gave him a confused look. "I feel horrible, but this one was so painful. Honestly, I'm scared to go through it again."

"Understandable. I don't have one on my ribs, but certain areas definitely hurt worse than others," he said. The back of his calf had been the worst for him by far.

"One day, when we have hours, you're going to have to tell me about all of yours," she laughed.

"It's a date," he replied. It almost sounded like that the date might not be within the two weeks she'd be there.

"Are you hungry?" she asked, "Let's go get something to eat."

CHAPTER NINE

Nicole lay on the bed in her hotel room, enjoying the air conditioning and hoping that she didn't look like a lobster from the day before with Derek. She was relieved that she better understood her feelings for Andrew now. Thinking things through on her run had helped her get some clarity. But she wasn't ready to call and tell him just yet. She didn't want to jump the gun. She wondered if that made her a bitch. For now, though, she was content that she'd come this far.

She had a to-do list prepared to make sure she saw each and every one of her father's favorite places. It made her feel accomplished. Her first dinner with Derek was amazing, so she had high hopes for dinner tonight. This restaurant was supposed to be the most famous in Puerto Vallarta. It was up the coast, high above the city, and was even in a famous movie. She couldn't quite recall which one. She'd have to ask Derek tonight.

She decided to wear the dress Derek had bought her on their walk along the Malecon the day before. He saw her reaction when she noticed it and had insisted she have it. Andrew had spoiled her at times, but it had never been a turn on like this. She hadn't realized it before, but weirdly it felt like a father indulging his daughter with presents. Somehow Derek made it sound like it was a present for him to see her in it. He grew up without a father, but someone taught him how to talk to women.

Nicole wasn't usually a jealous person. Still, she couldn't help wondering if he had bought that same dress for another woman before. He said he'd been there for a while. She couldn't remember how specific he had been. She was going to ask him more about his business at dinner. This relationship was starting to feel life-changing to her and before she got herself in too deep emotionally, she figured she better learn a little bit more about Derek Stone.

She glanced over at the clock: 4:15pm. She was going to meet him for drinks at his hotel this time. She had forty-five minutes to get ready. By the time she was ready, she had ten minutes to spare. She looked in the mirror to survey the results. The dress was a bit more daring than she would ever buy herself. It was the type of dress you see and think, *that would look fabulous on someone else.* Derek had begged her to try it on, said it was made for her.

It was a champagne color, with one thin strap over her shoulder. The back was practically nonexistent. The strap wrapped back under her arm almost like a bathing suit. The material came to an elegant knot almost at her tailbone, leaving her entire back bare. The dress was so long that it almost hit the floor. She got a pair of strappy high heels so that she wouldn't trip over the material when she walked. She kept her hair down, sweeping it over to one shoulder to show off the back of the dress, or lack thereof. She couldn't believe she was wearing this thing out in public. Still, she had to admit that it was flattering on her.

She felt extremely self-conscience when she stepped off the elevator. She did see a few heads turn and she hoped she didn't look like she was trying too hard. She was very glad it was such a neutral color and not bright red or something. She was relieved when she saw Derek leaning against the bar, watching her. His expression was worth all of the unease she felt about wearing the dress. He walked up to her, taking her hands in his and spreading them apart to admire her. He kissed her cheeks and whispered in her ear something about being the luckiest man in the world.

He immediately led her towards the street. Hector stopped to say hello to them both and tell Nicole how beautiful she looked. He said he would have the car ready for their dinner reservation. It was still bright out and she was instantly blinded when they walked out onto the sidewalk. Derek noticed and hurried them across the street to the cover of the lobby of his hotel.

When her full vision was restored, she realized that this hotel was much larger than it appeared from the outside. It was a rather small entrance that opened into a large courtyard with a quaint little bar and tables scattered about. She liked that Derek chose the bar over tables; it was always her preference as well.

"I had him chill a bottle of my favorite white wine," he told her as the bartender began to open a bottle when they sat down. She loved that Derek looked so tough, covered in tattoos, and yet enjoyed wine.

"I'd love a glass," she said. It was a Château Haut-Brion, again a very nice bottle. Andrew only drank red, so when they shared wine it was almost always a bottle of red. Nicole loved both. With all the sun she got during the day, a nice glass of crisp white sounded so refreshing.

"Fun fact about Nicole," she said after tasting the wine, "I'm a list maker." She pulled out a small piece of paper from her purse and showed Derek. "It's a list of all the things I still want to do and see. Tonight, we'll get to mark off another with dinner."

He reviewed the list and replied, "You let me know which ones where you'd like company and I'll be there." She had hoped he'd want to go with her. It would feel as if her dad would get to meet him.

"I can't really think of anywhere I'd need to be alone," she said, "I'd love for you to come."

He reached his hand behind her back and mindlessly rubbed along her bare skin. Even his touch could drive her crazy. If she had more guts, she would have told him they should skip dinner and go to his hotel room. She bit her tongue though. Not only was she not ready to say something like that to him, she really wanted to have dinner in this restaurant for her father.

This was already her fifth night in Mexico. Was she really prepared to go home in just over a week? She was pretty certain that she couldn't take any more time off of work, especially if she might be looking for an apartment by herself. And her boss, Nathan, would be sick of getting her column covered for any longer. Not like he would write any of them. That man could never make anything sound enjoyable and she had no faith that he could write about a wedding. She was surprised that he was ever passionate about journalism; he seemed to hate what he did. Maybe that happened when people get promoted above what they really enjoyed doing. That would never be her. She just wanted to write and leave all that other crap to someone else.

"Why the concerned look?" Derek asked, "What are you thinking about?" He moved his hand from the small of her back to brush a stray piece of hair out from her face. God, did everything that man do turn her on?

"I'm sorry, just thinking about work. Not ready to leave you or this paradise yet." She leaned over and softly kissed his lips. He used his tongue to slowly part hers. Perfectly in sync, she stood up and he parted his legs to pull her against his body. Luckily, there was only one other couple sitting at a table and they were off in their own world. But at this moment, Nicole wouldn't have cared if the entire place was packed with people. All she wanted was Derek.

This was so unlike her and she liked it. She kissed him deeply and passionately, trying to burn this moment into her brain forever. The kiss only lasted a minute or so, but she knew she'd remember it forever. She wasn't even sure why. The day had been fun and playful, but this was their first serious kiss since she had realized it was most likely over with Andrew. Even though she hadn't told Andrew yet, this kiss didn't feel like she was cheating on her boyfriend. Instead, it felt like she was kissing a boyfriend and that scared her a little.

She slowly leaned back to look at him. He was so incredibly handsome. She loved how he dressed. It was how she'd write "smart casual" if she needed to describe him as a guest at a wedding: off-white linen pants and a tattered-looking blue button-down shirt that could have been made specially to fit his body. Somehow he had mastered the beachwear look- casual but still dressed perfectly for dinner tonight.

The bartender walked up and set down a tray of different cheeses. Nicole loved cheese. Her motto in life could be "everything is better with cheese".

"These all go great with the wine," he said, "Try this one." He picked up a small piece of the cheese and lifted it to Nicole's mouth, again sexy as hell. "It's a goat cheese from Sancerre called Crottin de Chavignol considered the perfect pairing with this wine." Nicole tasted the sharpness of the cheese and then took a drink of the wine. She couldn't believe the difference. She loved the wine alone but with the cheese, it took on an entirely different taste, smooth and fabulous.

"Let's go to Napa sometime," she said without thinking.

"Anytime love, I will take you there," he snuck in a kiss on her cheek. *Wow, anytime?* She liked that.

They tried more of the cheeses with the wine and Derek helped explain how the different cheeses affected the taste of the wine on her palette. He told her that he had spent some time in Napa and knew the exact place to take her. This was a side of him that she hadn't expected. A Napa trip was always on the back burner with Andrew. They talked about it occasionally, but had never pulled the trigger to plan anything. Three years and nothing was planned, only days with Derek and he knew exactly where to take her. *This guy is exciting*, she thought to herself.

CHAPTER TEN

Derek had called ahead to the restaurant. Every table had a spectacular view, but they had one that was in a private gazebo, down a pathway from the main building and with a view of the water all around. Of anywhere in the world, it was by far one of his favorite places to eat. He wasn't surprised that Nicole's father had felt the same way. He did wish that he had met him in the past, but he was pretty positive that he hadn't. So far he sounded like someone he would have loved; he was sure he would have remembered him.

Hector had pulled the car up at exactly 7:00pm so that they could make the drive up the coast and be comfortably seated to watch the sun set. Derek couldn't wait to watch Nicole for the rest of the evening, to see how she soaked up the experience and remembered her father. He was a bit surprised at how important it was to him. Her happiness, especially on this level, was vital to him. "Hector, how is everyone at your hotel?" he inquired. He was only concerned about how one little woman in particular was doing; he hoped that Hector understood the question.

"*Bien, Señor* Derek. I heard employees complimenting your Nicole's dress." Hector gave him a sly look in the rear-view mirror and Derek realized that Silvia had either seen or heard about him picking Nicole up at the hotel. He was still nervous that Silvia would confront her if she was able to catch her alone. He knew he should give Nicole fair warning, but didn't want to chance ruining their night.

Derek watched Nicole as she looked out the window over the extreme contrast in the scenery. To her right, outside her window was the gorgeous blue water. Then she would lean slightly and look out his side of the car and see more green than one could ever see, except in Ireland. The road climbed higher and higher the further they drove. Finally, they arrived at the restaurant. It seemed to pop out of nowhere from the middle of a jungle to a cliff at the edge of the water.

The restaurant looked like it was almost entirely outside. There were several large gazebo-style covers over the majority of the tables. Everything from the floors to the covers was made from beautiful wood and it seemed to stretch over the water. There was soft lighting dangling down (the steel stars with little holes all over that were such a popular decoration in Puerto Vallarta) and candles lit at each table. A popular decoration in Puerto Vallarta is steel starts with light inside and little holes all over. They were hanging everywhere around the restaurant and it all looked magical.

Nicole had the most genuine smile on her face. She was surprised when the hostess led them off the large patio and down a set of stairs.

"Where are we going?" she asked him, leaning close.

"You need to experience this restaurant from their best table," he told her. She squeezed his hand hard and squealed when they came around the corner and saw the gazebo lit up with stars hanging everywhere from different heights and white party lights lining the gazebo pillars and cover. The single table inside was covered with a crisp white table cloth.

"I thought we'd have an after dinner drink at the bar so that you can spend some time in the main restaurant as well," he added. She looked up at him and kissed his cheek.

"Thank you! This is absolutely perfect." She practically ran up the steps to the table, as fast as she could without tripping on her long dress. Derek darted after her, laughing, to make sure she didn't end up falling. He pulled out her chair and allowed her to sit before going across to his own. One more time, as if by magic, wine arrived immediately at the table. This time he chose a bold red to go with the rich food the chef would prepare. He also asked it to arrive with two tall mixed drinks.

"I remembered that you like Crown & Sevens. I thought we'd take our time and enjoy both," he told her, "Do you recall a dish your father liked best or shall we take a look at the menu?" Derek motioned toward where they were stacked on the table.

"I know he ordered a sea bass all the time, but not sure if they have more than one," she said as she picked one up.

"Take a look, but I'm pretty sure I know exactly what he ordered," he replied. He had had their sea bass numerous times and knew that locals loved it as well.

"Which one is it?" she asked.

"They have a ginger soy lacquered Chilean sea bass over a bed of sautéed vegetables. Other than Night at the Iguana, it's what they are known for. "

"That's the movie, I meant to ask you," she said excitedly, "I remember my father calling me from one of his trips to Vallarta and telling me I had to go rent it." She seemed as though she was going to continue on

83

the topic, but her mind suddenly veered off in another direction. "Employees were talking about my dress? That is so embarrassing!" She rolled her eyes and put her head in her hands for a moment.

He immediately regretted asking Hector in front of her. He had just been nervous about Silvia since that morning. He didn't mean to embarrass her. But Silvia had the potential to ruin this relationship if she said the wrong thing.

"No, love, it's not embarrassing," he reassured her, "I'm sure they were admiring you or wishing they were you." He reached across the table for her hands and she instinctively put them into his. She rolled her eyes again, probably at the thought of other women wishing they were her. He loved that part about her. She wasn't insecure, but also wasn't conceited. She walked a fine line between the two and did it very well.

They stayed like that until the server arrived. Derek checked with Nicole first and then ordered them both the sea bass.

"Is this your first time your company has sent you to Puerto Vallarta?" Nicole inquired.

"Oh no. Like your father, I travel quite frequently," he said, still holding back just a bit, though he wasn't sure why anymore.

"Where is your favorite place?" she asked.

"That is a tough one." Derek thought about the question. He loved places for different reasons. Puerto Vallarta may be at the top of his list now for sentimental reasons. Not only was Stone Hospitality, Inc. born there, but now he had met Nicole there as well.

"I love Italy, though work hasn't taken me there yet," he finally answered.

"I've always wanted to see Venice," she said, eyes bright.

"You would love it. I haven't been there in over five years. We're due for a trip, huh?" He needed a filter with Nicole. The things he said to her before he had a chance to think would never cease to amaze him. She just laughed and took a drink of wine. Planning international travel may be moving just tad fast, even he could admit that. "Too fast?" he asked.

"A little, but it's sweet that you're planning," she replied. He wasn't exactly sure how to take that answer. Had she spoken to the Maybe Boyfriend? The thought hadn't occurred to him until this moment. He could feel his blood starting to boil and he knew he had to get a check on his temper. She did seem open to a Napa trip, so it might be that somewhere as far as Italy seemed a little crazy, five days into a relationship. It was crazy; he knew it himself.

He decided to change the subject so things didn't get weird. "How did your phone call go with your friend this morning?" he asked. He tried not to sound like he was prying, though the idea that she might have called the Maybe Boyfriend was still floating around in his head.

"You would think I've been missing for a month!" she laughed and he waited for her to continue "She left me so many voicemails and text messages. She ended up thinking I was mad at her. She understood why I left, but Kate is the worrying type."

"She's glad you're safe then?" he prompted her to tell more.

"Yes…" She seemed to be considering telling him something and he could feel his blood pressure start to rise.

"I told her about you." And without giving him a chance to respond, she went on as if she felt the need to explain herself, "She was worried that I was here by myself and said she would have come. I wanted her to know I wasn't alone." She gave him the sweetest smile.

"First, no, love, you're not alone. And second, were you concerned I wouldn't like that you told her?"

"No, it's not that. I don't really know why…oh, I don't know." Her face reddened and she shook her head.

"What is it?" He really couldn't tell what she was thinking.

She sighed and closed her eyes to block out seeing him. "I'm worried it sounded like I was telling her about my new boyfriend. I don't want to scare you off." She opened her eyes enough to peek through her lids at him.

All in one moment, a plethora of thoughts ran through his head. Would he have liked her to call him her boyfriend? What did she really think about their relationship only five days in? Was this just a vacation fling? Would she go back to the Maybe Boyfriend? Would Derek recover if she did? Did she want to say it was serious?

"What did you tell her?" he asked, picking her hand up and kissing it tenderly so she'd know that he wasn't at all upset that she had mentioned him.

"I told her that I met someone and it was intense," she told him. He assumed that was a quick synopsis of what she really said.

"Intense is a pretty accurate way to put this," he said with a grin. He wanted to ask about the Maybe Boyfriend, but wasn't sure if he should. Luckily, she kept talking.

"She thinks that my father may have sent you to me." A look of embarrassment came over her face. "Kate isn't the hearts and flowers type either. It seemed rather out of character for her, but I did like the idea."

"I do too," was all he was able to say before the server arrived with their food covered in a domed silver cover to keep it warm from his walk to the gazebo.

He could tell immediately that Nicole was happy with the selection. Her eyes practically rolled into the back of her head when she took the first bite of the fish. "I'm not even a fish person!" she said.

"Can I try to make you look that satisfied tonight?" he teased.

"It's no contest," she smiled at him.

"Who wins? Is it me or the sea bass?" he joked with her again.

"You all the way, baby," she laughed.

They ate their dinner and talked more about their pasts. She asked a little bit about his childhood and he was more open with her than any other person in his life. A close second would be Gael. He knew that for the business' sake there were parts of his personality that should be explained. He told her about seeing his mother do drugs and moving from apartment to apartment whenever she'd get evicted. His accountant sent her a small amount of money each month, but he was completely removed from the situation. He knew his mother well enough not to send too much. He knew she'd spend it on drugs.

He didn't get into any of that with Nicole, not tonight. He always figured that if he did end up with a wife, she would know everything about it and that taking care of his mother was a necessary evil. He couldn't leave her to live on the streets or sell her body. She may have been a horrible mother, but she was still just that, his mother.

They each finished their plates. Nicole suggested they have some dessert at the bar with their drinks, so he suggested an apple dessert that he knew she would love. He took her hand and led her up to the bar. She stopped just shy of walking into the restaurant and turned to look at the view. She leaned into the crook of his shoulder and was still for a moment. He figured she was thinking of her father. He rubbed the bare skin on her back and let her tell him when she was ready. Time would stand still for as long as she needed.

In that moment, he had a longing that he thought he'd squashed in the fighting cage- a wish that he had a father. He didn't like thinking that, didn't like needing him. He hated the universe for taking Nicole's from her. Why couldn't his waste of a father die in a car accident instead? Maybe he had, Derek thought. He had no idea if the man was alive or dead.

Nicole leaned up and kissed his cheek; it had become the cutest little habit. Wordlessly, they walked up to the bar. Just as he was about to order, he received a text message. He checked his phone to see if it was Gael. It was from Silvia: "I see you took your blond out again tonight. I'll miss seeing you leave her hotel shirtless again tomorrow.'" Derek did not reply. This was just what he was worried would happen. He still planned on having her job if she dared approach Nicole, especially without him there. But he would deal with Silvia another time. He was determined not to let this ruin their time tonight.

He ordered the apple tartlet and another bottle of the same red wine; if they didn't finish it at the bar, they could take it back to the hotel. As he had that thought, he realized he was picturing his apartment at the Paraíso. He thought about the day he met Nicole and it felt like it might be his fourth life-changing moment. It wasn't very clear to him now if it was when he was sitting at the bar at the Playa Vallarta and first saw her or if it was now, in this moment, at the bar in this restaurant. But he knew it was life changing. He wanted to take her to his apartment at the hotel and let her see the personal life he had created. He wanted to tell her everything.

CHAPTER ELEVEN

The apple dessert arrived and it was divine, just like everything that night. She sat at the bar, eating and looking over at Derek as he spoke to the restaurant manager. He really did know everyone in this town. Who was he?

She had discovered more about his past tonight. This man had overcome so much since he had been the poor little boy who had no father and a mother that sounded too selfish to put her needs aside to take care of a helpless child. And look at him now. She wasn't quite sure of his success at the moment, but any amount was amazing, given his circumstances. This man was the one that needed a lotus flower tattooed on his skin, not her. She smiled at the thought of a flower, even a simple drawing like hers, mixed in with all those masculine designs.

How successful was he? Who exactly did he work for? She hadn't noticed until now that he had been rather vague about why he was here. It wasn't because she was disinterested. She supposed it was because they had so much to learn about each other. Somehow they always got onto another topic. Was that on purpose? She inspected him again wondering if he was some type of undercover agent. As far-fetched as it seemed, she wouldn't be surprised at all if that's who he really was. Would she ever know?

Nicole hadn't noticed that while she was pondering all of this, she had slowly eaten far more than her half of the dessert. It was so good, she couldn't stop herself. She set down her fork and let Derek finish his conversation. He must have been waiting for her to do so because as soon as she did, he introduced her to the man with whom he was talking.

"Manuel, this is *mi amor*, Nicole." She didn't miss his reference. She liked it.

"*Hola, Señorita* Nicole, are you enjoying yourself this evening?" He lifted her hand and kissed it quickly.

"Thank you, yes. Your place is wonderful," she said and leaned in toward Derek slightly. She had been able to tell over the few short days that he had a protective side. She guessed that even with a simple hello kiss on the hand, she should let Manuel see that she was his. Derek's way never came across controlling or domineering, just protective. As she leaned, he put his arm around her to show that he appreciated the gesture.

"I will leave you two to enjoy your evening. We will talk again, Derek, and I hope to see you soon, *Señorita* Nicole," Manuel said politely. They both said their goodbyes and he was off to check on other guests.

Nicole saw Derek raise his eyebrow at her when he noticed the remaining dessert. "I tried to leave you some," Nicole said with a laugh.

"It is quite all right," he said as they each picked up their forks and continued eating.

"Do you come here often?" she asked. She was determined to find out a little bit more about his travels, but she had a feeling she couldn't be too pushy about it. There may be a reason he had been vague.

"I usually come up for dinner at least a couple of times while I am here. Vallarta is rather small, so it's very easy to become a regular and be recognized. Tourism is this city's life line so the locals make sure to remember those that return." Again she noticed that he was talking more about Vallarta than himself. He might be very skilled at avoiding these questions, but why? She wondered if she should come right out and ask if he was some super-secret spy. She would never tell anyone. Well, probably Kate. Hmmm, maybe he shouldn't tell her anything. What in the world was wrong with her? She had fallen for a guy practically the second she saw him and now she was turning him into James Bond.

"Would you like to see any more of downtown this evening?" he asked her, "There are some beautiful rooftop bars along the Malecon." Nicole was somewhat of a night owl to an extent, but she didn't really enjoy staying out till all hours of the morning like she had in her twenties. Once she turned thirty, things changed and she enjoyed getting to bed by midnight. She wondered if Derek was the type that was at after hour clubs all the time.

"It's after ten and we still have the drive back," she said after checking her watch, "Could we go tomorrow night? Maybe get an earlier start?"

"Of course." Luckily, he didn't seem to be disappointed.

"How will we get back?" she said, remembering that they were in the middle of nowhere.

"Hector is still outside," he told her.

Poor Hector, he had been waiting this entire time. "What?!" She hadn't realized how loudly she said that and consciously lowered her voice. "Should we invite him in or order him food?" She knew she sounded worried.

"You are very sweet," he replied, "It's what drivers do for this restaurant. It's more time and gas to go back and then return. When we go outside, you'll see a line of cars and taxis along the side of the place. The drivers hang out and usually bet on cards or dice while they wait. From what I can gather from Hector, he is very good and makes more money playing than I pay him to drive us." That made her feel better, but she was still concerned he'd be hungry. Before she could ask about ordering him food again, Derek continued. "You do not need to worry about food. The restaurant is very nice about bringing out some food for the drivers while they wait. When I come, I order them all something more exciting from the menu. Manuel will have plenty boxed up for them."

"That's very nice. Do you try and expense that?" she laughed, half kidding, knowing there was no way he could turn in a receipt for numerous specials on top of what he ordered.

With a chuckle, he responded, "No, I don't expense these types of dinners." Still a rather elusive answer, she thought.

"What does your company do here? You said their life line was tourism," she mentioned. She hoped he didn't think she was being too nosy. If he was in fact James Bond, she was sure he'd have a cover story anyway.

"It's in the hotel industry actually. Similar to your father, I visit the locations. But I'm not on the computer or technology side of things." She decided not to pry any further into what the company did. He had given her something.

"How long will you be here in Vallarta?" That was a reasonable question, she thought.

"As long as I feel the need to stay or if I decide I'd like to see another location," he replied, rather reluctantly. She was ready to change the subject for his sake, but he continued, "It is going to be rather dull here once you return to Chicago." He looked genuinely disappointed at that thought.

"Didn't you say there was a chance you might be able to come to Chicago?" she asked hopefully. The idea of not seeing Derek again would kill her.

"Yes, my meeting this morning was regarding that exact topic. It's going very well," he told her and kissed her lips. This man could unnerve her with one touch.

"Whew, so we can see each other when you come?" she said, trying not to sound needy. The idea of him sometimes being in Chicago made this all seem more possible. She could visit him in Detroit when he was there. Or maybe one of his other vacation spots. Could they really make this work?

"I will find any reason I can to be in Chicago. Or maybe I'll take you with me around the world," he snuck that last part in and she wondered if he was testing the waters to see her response.

"I've been meaning to do that one day, travel the world," she said jokingly. The mention of Venice just hours ago did seem soon.

Nicole looked around the restaurant. There were only two tables still occupied by guests. One was a large table in the corner that looked like a family traveling together. The other was a couple that could easily be on their honeymoon. All of the other bar guests had left. Deciding to be bold again, she stood up and put her arms around Derek's neck. He spread his legs and allowed her to lean the weight of her body into him. She looked straight into his eyes and, before she kissed him, told him to take her to her hotel room. She chose not to use the words "make love", just in case. She left what they would do up to his imagination.

She took the lead on this kiss and he seemed to savor it. She started slowly, kissing on his lower lip and slowly searching his mouth with her tongue. The kiss deepened, as if it were out of their control, and when it did, he was in power again. He pushed his body toward her and her back arched back slightly. She matched his hunger with her own. The feeling of his hands on her back was all she could bear. She reached up and rubbed her hands along his extremely short hair. It felt like her hands were touching velvet. She was worried that with the twenty-minute drive back to her hotel, Hector would be getting quite the show. She slowed them down as best she could. They were still in a restaurant, for goodness' sake.

"I want to take you to my hotel," he said after the break in their kiss.

"Take me now," she answered breathlessly.

"I want to make love to you in their rooftop pool under the moonlight." It was so romantic. Andrew didn't know how to say things like that. She couldn't really remember anyone saying such things and she was surprised at how much it affected her. Her body began to melt in his arms as he kissed her again. He kissed her cheeks, her ears, her neck, continuing to talk through the kisses. "Let me show you my life," he whispered. She didn't really understand what he meant, but then again, everything was hazy from his touch.

Without a thought about whether the bill had been paid, she grabbed her little purse and pulled him up off the chair toward the front door. She felt empowered by him; she wasn't at all self-conscious about her dress or kissing him in public. She wanted him to see how much she desired him.

Hector was leaning against his car, chatting with the last two drivers outside. He saw them coming out the door, hand-in-hand, and jumped into the car, circling it around to the front door. She could never get over how quickly he could move his little body. Next thing she knew, he was opening the back door for them. When they were all settled, he pulled onto the road and headed toward the Romantic Zone. He didn't say a word to them. He must have felt their need for each other and was giving them their moment.

"Thank you, Hector," she said finally, "We'll do our best to keep it clean back here." She laughed and leaned into Derek for another kiss.

CHAPTER TWELVE

Derek led Nicole down the hall to his apartment at the Paraíso. Everything felt like it was happening in slow motion. He was trying to grasp the enormity of this moment for him. After all these years, he had finally found someone he was willing to share this part of himself with. No woman had ever been in one of his apartments.

When they arrived at the door, he took Nicole's face in his hands. He wasn't sure how to articulate to her what this moment meant but he tried with, "I have never brought a woman to this room." He could tell that she wasn't exactly sure why he had told her that, so he continued, "For the past ten years, this has been my room whenever I've come here." With that, he opened the door and let her walk in.

She hadn't seen a regular room at The Paraíso, but she would immediately know it was different. The rest of the hotel, like most of Vallarta, was very colorful and traditional. Walls and tiles were decorated with vibrant colors. Derek's personal apartment was the complete opposite. Everything was clean and white. It was the size of two rooms that were combined to one larger apartment style space. There was a small but modern eat-in kitchen and a living room with floor-to-ceiling windows that opened to a large patio running the length of the apartment. The floor tiles were almost white with grey lines marbled throughout. There was a sleek charcoal-colored contemporary styled couch that looked like one big rectangle, white marble coffee table with a big black bowl that held the remote control and, hanging on the wall, an enormous television, far bigger than what was standard for most hotels. Above the couch was a contemporary painting of the ocean. The bedroom had the same floor-to-ceiling wall of windows. His bed was an oversized California king with stark white bedding and a mountain of pillows. The bathroom was updated with all of the amenities. It was his little hidden treasure in the middle of an ancient Mexican town. And he was ready to share it all with her.

He kept a close eye on Nicole as she slowly walked in and looked around.

"What's going on Derek? Do you live here?" She gave him a questioning look.

"I do, occasionally." He hadn't really thought about how to explain everything. "I started a company about fifteen years ago. I came up with the idea when I was sitting on the exact barstool where I met you," he smiled, "We buy properties in expanding vacation spots and hang on to them until we sell at a premium. One of my stipulations is an apartment at my disposal at each location. So you could say, I live a lot of places."

Nicole stood in the living room and slowly spun around to see everything from that one spot. Derek couldn't quite get a read on what she was thinking. She looked like she wasn't sure either. She was probably trying to take it all in.

"Why have you never brought anyone here?" she asked quietly.

"I have no interest in women that want me for my money," he said plainly, "I learned quickly with the UFC fighting that there are lots of women that will want you for your power and money. This world is far from that life, but I was fortunate enough to find success again. With fighting, I couldn't keep my success to myself. With this, I can." He hoped that made sense to her. He walked over and she wrapped her arms around his neck.

"Thank you for bringing me here," was all she said and then they quietly stood in his apartment. Derek's shoulders and back relaxed immediately as he felt an overwhelming sense of relief. He hadn't even noticed how tense his body had been.

"Come see my view," he told her, "The only person who's seen it, besides the staff, is Gael. He's not nearly as fun as you." He kissed her lips quickly and led her to the door. He opened it and continued to slide it into the next window panel, moving them over until the entire wall of windows was gone. The living room now grew to twice its size as it continued out to the balcony. He had the same contemporary style furniture out there: a table, chairs, and a large wicker chaise lounge big enough for them both to sunbath on during the day. He imagined sunbathing on it with Nicole and then, looking over at her, realized how much he wanted to make love on it as well.

She walked over to the railing, taking in the full view. She looked at home there and he wanted to commission someone to paint the scene and hang it on his wall. He already knew of the perfect gallery on the Malecon, with local artists. She was standing there in the first of many beautiful dresses he would buy her, her long hair blowing softly in the wind while she looked out, with the black sky and the moon with millions of stars behind her. It was a perfect moment.

"It's kind of sad thinking of you up here alone all these years," she said. Most women would be happy to know he hadn't shared that bed with another woman. Nicole was different; she was able to take herself out of the situation and see that he had been lonely. What was he going to do when she was gone? He may never return to Puerto Vallarta again without her. He couldn't imagine walking back out onto this balcony and not seeing her there.

"It won't be lonely up here anymore." He walked up to her and put her face in his hands again. He kissed her lips slowly. He wanted to savor this moment. He wanted to make love to her all over his apartment. He saw her look up out of the corner of her eyes.

"Don't worry. No one can see from their balconies. I insisted on privacy." He grabbed the hair at the back of her neck again and pulled. The sound she made in the water that day had been burned in his brain. He wanted to hear that moan again and he wanted to make her moan louder. When he kissed her neck, he heard that sound and he was instantly hard. He slipped the thin strap of her dress over her shoulder and it fell to the ground around her feet. She stood there naked with only her long blond hair and her strappy little heels for company. She smiled at him and he realized this could be a cover photo for an issue of *Playboy*. She began to unbutton his shirt, letting it slip off his shoulders. She undid his pants and they dropped to his feet. He immediately kicked off his shoes, knowing there was no way that he could look as sexy as she did with nothing on but high heels.

He grabbed the backs of her thighs and lifted her off the ground. She wrapped her legs around him and began kissing his neck. He walked her over to the chaise lounge and they both landed together with him on top of her. He kissed her slowly all over her body. Their first time together, there had been so much passion and built up tension that they moved rather quickly. Now he was going to take his time and satisfy her all over.

He kissed her shoulders and arm and found one of her breasts. Nicole arched her back at the sensation and he heard her moan again. He took his time teasing her body and he could feel goose bumps forming on her arms. That made him more excited. But he was determined to hear that moan over and over before he was inside of her. He moved down to her flat stomach, tanned from their days on the beach. He kissed the side of her hip bone and she squirmed into him. He spread her legs apart; he couldn't wait to taste her. He quickly found what she needed. She lifted her hips up and grabbed his head. When he heard her sighs and she called out his name, he gently kissed the inside of her thigh. Then he kissed all over her body again, moving himself back up to look into her eyes as he slid inside of her.

It really had never been like this for him before. He always knew the difference between fucking and making love. When he was with a woman, more often than not they just wanted to fuck. And when it was slower, it never had the passion that he felt right now. He knew just how to make her moan louder and loved that he had that effect on her. He enjoyed that as long as he could until he no longer could control his body. He pulled out at the last minute and his body fell on top of her.

After a few minutes of her kissing his shoulder and neck, he grabbed a towel that he kept folded near the chaise and cleaned them both up. He lay back flat and closed his eyes. She curled her body up to him. It still seemed so strange, how their bodies interacted like they had been together their whole lives. She was tracing his arms along one of his tattoos. It went up one shoulder and down the other.

"It's still pretty early. Tell me about your tattoos," she said sweetly.

"The one you're looking at now, that was my first. In Latin it means, 'a life lived in fear is a life half lived'." It went up one shoulder and down the other.

"I like that," she smiled.

"After I found MMA fighting, I had the boxing gloves tattooed on my calf." He turned his leg out so she could see the tattoo that covered the entire muscle. "This one was like your rib cage. It took me two sittings to get it done. Never felt pain like that in my life." He laughed at the memory.

"My next was the Maori design that takes up this shoulder. An artist friend of mine designed it for me." Derek had made sure that it flowed well with the Latin letters but didn't cover them. He pointed to his other shoulder. "This one was my fourth. The compass represents all the travelling I do with my company. The name of the company is hidden here in the design." He showed her where it read "Stone Hospitality" intertwined in the patterns, elaborate but still masculine. Each tattoo was separate, but they all flowed into each other with a similar motif in the background.

"This one," he pointed to the circular figure on his chest, "Is a Buddhist mandala for strength." It reminded her of American Indian art. "It reminds me to look for my inner strength and to fight for what I deserve," he said, "I've always considered myself spiritual rather than religious. All of the religions, for the most part, have some of it figured out. If you put them all together, you could lead a pretty good life."

He leaned so she could see his back. "This one going down between my shoulder blades, what does it look like to you?"

"Some kind of design." She touched the tattoo while she looked at it and he wanted to take her again right there.

"It's an ambigram. Do you know what that is?" he asked.

"Sounds kind of familiar but no," she answered honestly.

"Look at from the left and then the right."

She cocked her head. "It reads friend," she read aloud. Then she turned her head the other direction and practically yelled, "It reads enemy! I love this!" She kept turning her head back and forth like it was magic.

"For my entire life, the majority of my fighting had been for profit or money to survive," he explained, "I had to fight friends and guys that were good people. None of them were based on emotions, none of them were based on hatred. They were my friends but I'd step in the cage and I'd need to see them as my enemy."

"This one may be my favorite of your tattoos. Although this one," she pointed to the Maori design his friend had drawn, "I like because I can see it the best when you're on top of me."

They both laughed. He could tell that she was a bit embarrassed to admit that, which was cute as hell. He looked out into the night with Nicole's head on his shoulder. Everything felt right in his world. Nicole was meant to be here with him.

He thought about her father for a moment. Could her friend Kate have been right? Was it possible that her father knew that the Maybe Boyfriend wasn't right for her? Derek didn't have a normal life, but Nicole needed more than normal. He knew that he wanted to take care of her, always. She would never want for anything. His mind went back to the question he asked himself earlier that day. Did he just want normalcy or did he really want Nicole herself? He looked down at her naked body draped over him. A man would be insane not to want it. But she was so much more than that. Maybe he needed to be ready to want normalcy before he met her. The universe worked in amazing ways, bringing them together at the perfect moment in both of their lives.

"Tell me about fighting," she stated simply.

"Before UFC, the fighting was pretty normal. Nothing was very structured. I was a teenager, about sixteen, when I started fighting for real money. Well, real money for me. I'd make a thousand dollars with a hundred people watching and betting on me." He kissed her head before he continued, "UFC was an entirely different world. There were rules and regulations, weight classes, fancy locker rooms and cagess. But it was a crazy lifestyle. So many times I felt like I was living like a rock star. In the cage, it was extremely regulated, but what went on in the background felt like the backstage of a concert. I won't go into the dirty details for you. But I saw some crazy things."

"Was it hard to leave that life?" she asked.

"Not one bit. I wasn't very comfortable with the attention. I held the title in the welterweight class, the one in between light and middle weight, for quite a while. It was weird seeing my picture online or my name in lights. Watching myself fight on TV was especially strange." He thought for a moment. "It always seemed like an out-of-body experience. Like I was watching myself live the life, but I wasn't present in it. It set me up financially to start this company, but leaving the cage was easy." He never talked about this with anyone, so he hadn't quite realized before why it had been easy to leave. "I like this life much better," he stated, "I didn't like when someone would recognize me. I enjoy having all the perks of the money and no one realizing it. It's my own little secret."

"Hector driving you around makes sense now," she said.

"Yes, this is a sister hotel to Playa Vallarta so they are very nice to me over there," he told her, "I have a deal with Victor, the general manager. I double Hector's salary and he is at my disposal. It helps take care of his family."

"You are very generous," she kissed his cheek.

"I fought for everything I had; I like to help make it easier for some." He found her mouth and kissed her deeply before whispering, "I want to take you inside and make love to you in my bed. It's been waiting patiently for you."

CHAPTER THIRTEEN

Nicole woke up surrounded by a mountain of white. The sheets on Derek's bed had to be about a million thread count because they were the most comfortable things she had ever felt. She looked around, letting her eyes adjust to the light. Her face lit up when she realized that the windows here opened up like the ones in the living room. There was water for as far as she could see and she could hear the sound of the ocean waves crashing into the sand. It made her feel like she had been sleeping out on the beach. Listening for Derek, she heard him moving around in the kitchen just as she noticed the smell of breakfast cooking. How in the world did she get so lucky?

Most men kept their boxers and t-shirts in the top drawers of their dressers; Nicole opened one of Derek's and found what she was looking for. Hoping he wouldn't mind, she slipped into a crisp white t-shirt and a pair of blue plaid boxers that clung to her hips for dear life. She wandered into the kitchen. He was at the stove, his back to her while he attended to what smelled like eggs. He wore only a pair of board shorts which made him look incredibly sexy. She smiled at the tattoo on his back, now easily seeing the friend and enemy blended together. Sneaking up behind him, she reached her arms around his bare waist. He turned around and hugged her so that her feet lifted up off the floor.

"I hope you don't mind, I thought I'd look a tad fancy in my dress this morning," she looked down at the clothes that she was wearing.

"Love, you can wear my clothes anytime you'd like. They look much more appealing on you." He kissed her lips. "Are you hungry?"

"Yes, it smells wonderful," she replied. She sat at the little table and he grabbed two plates out of the cabinet. "Can I help with anything?" she asked.

"Nope, everything is ready; I got us both lattes as well." He grabbed two to-go cups, emblazoned with the name of the café downstairs, and put them on the table in front of her. "I had Hector pick them up along with something for you to wear back to your room." He handed her the bag from the counter. "He has pretty good taste," he smiled and took a drink of his coffee.

Nicole peeked into the bag- a simple blue sundress. Given that she didn't have a bra, she was glad it wasn't white. "Thank you," she smiled and took a sip of the coffee. Derek brought over their plates, each with a slice of toast spread with well-peppered avocado and a heap of scrambled eggs with cheese sprinkled on top. Everything looked wonderful. She loved avocado but had never tried it this way. When she took a bite, she never wanted to eat toast without it again.

"Old habits die hard," he told her, "I still start my day with a healthy breakfast."

"I've never had this," she replied as she took another bite of the toast, "I love it."

It felt so natural to be eating breakfast with him at the tiny table in this gorgeous apartment. She thought for a moment about that word, yes she guessed it was an apartment. Hotel room didn't really sound right. They chatted as they finished their breakfast. Derek told her he'd walk her back to the hotel. He needed to talk with Victor about a few things and then they could go through her list of her father's places. Derek had already showered so she could get ready while he had his quick meeting and then he was all hers for the day. Immediately she started thinking about what she would like to do first. Definitely the Kings Head Pub. They could try a heavy British beer and maybe they'd even have some British food. An authentic English breakfast would be out since they just ate, but maybe they could try that another day. "I know exactly where I'd like to go," she said enthusiastically, "The King's Head Pub, isn't it close by?"

He had been rinsing the dishes and stood still there for a second. He walked over to her with the water still running. "Oh love, I'm sorry but the King's Head closed quite a few years back."

She tried to hide her disappointment, but he could tell she was upset. He pulled her up from the chair and wrapped her arms around his neck. "It was turned into a little breakfast place. If I had known, I would have taken you there this morning."

She tried to interrupt, to tell him it wasn't his fault, but he stopped her with a kiss on the lips. "How about I take you there so you can see where it was and we'll have an early lunch," he offered, "They do have a nice brunch menu. I'll show you where everything was when it was the King's Head. You can imagine it in your mind."

"What happened to the owner?" she asked, "That was my favorite story from my dad's travels. He came over for a vacation, fell in love with the town, went back, sold everything, and opened a bar here." A wave of emotion overtook her body. She wanted to cry and she didn't really know why. She couldn't believe this was affecting her so much. She missed saying goodbye to her dad and now she missed seeing this place.

"Do you want to meet him?" Derek said with a smile on his face, "He was ready to retire from the bar business and spend more time in England with his grandchildren. When he couldn't find someone that wanted to keep the concept of a British pub, he sold it. He spends the English winters here and the summers across the pond. He hasn't left for home yet."

"You know him, too? Of course you do, you seem to know everyone," she laughed and wiped away a tear.

"I told you, this is a small town." He kissed her cheek. "I'll have Gael track him down and we'll have a drink with him while you're here."

"Thank you," she smiled, "I'm going to get dressed."

Derek held her hand as they walked across the cobblestone street. He kissed her cheek when they reached the door and told her he'd meet her by the bar when she was ready. She saw him stop to talk with Hector on his way to the office and laughed to herself, wondering what errand he was going to send him on now.

When Nicole stepped off the elevator, the sun was blinding. It was early enough that it hadn't reached high enough in the sky to be blocked by the building. She didn't have her sunglasses, so she tried her best to cover herself from the rays with her hand. Though it was early, it was already hot out and the air felt stagnant. She was reaching to pull her room key out of her purse when out of nowhere something crashed her head against the stone wall. A massive forearm came from behind and closed around her neck and tightened. She grabbed at the arm, digging her nails in as hard as she could and kicking her legs, but the grip only tightened.

Nicole was sweating, her hair tangled in her face and sticking to her neck. Her attacker licked her cheek and started talking in Spanish as she struggled. She was so disoriented from the blow that she could barely stay on her feet. Half out of her mind with fear, she screamed for Derek as loud as she could before the man hit her in the side of the head to shut her up. He was incredibly strong, but she was determined to get away from him. She tried to stay aware of her surroundings. She could see part of his upper arm. There was a tattoo; it looked something like a feather.

He must have grabbed her key when she took it out of her purse because he was opening the door with one hand, while his other arm was secure around her throat. Everything was starting to fade in and out. Her head was pounding and she was seeing stars, but she reached anywhere she could, trying to find something of his she could grab onto. Her father had always told her to gouge the eyes, so she threw back her arms, searching for his head. She screamed again as he began dragging her into the room. He threw her hard, face-down on the bed. She began to cry. She was not prepared for this to happen; she didn't know if she would ever recover from the trauma of it all.

He held her down by her neck and she heard what sounded like his pants unzipping. Nicole closed her eyes tight, trying to block everything out.

The next thing she heard was loud a growl and a crash. Instantly, she was free. She scrambled up the bed and turned around. It was Derek, on top of the man and hitting him with so much force that it seemed like the ground shook with each blow. Another man ran in the room and she guessed it might be Victor, the general manager. The body underneath Derek was lifeless, but he wasn't letting up. Victor ran up and pulled Derek off, crying, "Stop, you will kill him!"

"Exactly," Derek yelled, trying to get back to the body now lying on the floor.

"Go take care of her," Victor said, "I will take this piece of shit to the *policía*."

Derek looked like he was in a trance. But with the mention of Nicole, he came back to reality. She was still crying and curled up in a ball on the bed. He sat down, pulling her body on top of his and holding her like she was a baby. She sobbed uncontrollably while he rubbed her back. He gently lifted her head by her chin to examine her face. She was so grateful that he had come to her room. Had he heard her scream?

"How did you know?" she asked between sobs.

"I heard the scream," he said, "I knew instantly it was you. I will make sure you never have to scream for me like that ever again. I will always protect you." He tenderly touched the huge bump on the side of her forehead.

"I'm so glad you did. Derek, I don't think I could have survived what was about to happen. The asshole licked my neck. He licked my neck!" She started crying again and he rocked her in his lap.

"I'm going to take you to my apartment and I'll have a doctor come check you out."

He picked her up and she let him, not caring if she looked like an idiot being carried like a child through a hotel lobby. She didn't care about anything but him. She leaned her head against him as he took her down the stairs. She could hear lots of commotion from behind an employee area and figured her attacker was probably being held in that room. She closed her eyes when they reached the lobby so that she didn't have to see how many people were staring. She heard the sound of sirens arriving and a man ran up to Derek. Without stopping, Derek told him her room number.

When they reached his apartment, he gently set her down to open the door. She walked slowly over to the couch. Contrary to its modern shape, it was much more comfortable than it looked. She thought it would feel like a slab of concrete. She curled into the corner and closed her eyes. Derek sat down beside her and asked how badly she hurt.

She tried to speak without crying. "I have a horrible headache and I must have a black eye, but other than that, I'm just scared out of my mind."

"The doctor should be here soon," he told her.

"Who was that guy?" she wondered aloud, "I tried to do what they always tell you. I tried to find an identifying thing about him." She closed her eyes again at the memory of what had happened. "He had a tattoo on his right arm. It looked kind of like a feather."

She saw everything in Derek go abruptly tense, eyes wide and his back straightened. He reached for his phone and sent a text.

"What is it? Do you know him?" she started getting extremely uneasy. Her breathing picked up. It felt like she was going to have a panic attack. "Who was that?" she was practically yelling now.

Just as Derek opened his mouth, the doctor arrived and Nicole was relieved to see it was a woman. She didn't think she could handle a strange man near her right now. The doctor was wearing a white coat embroidered with the hotel logo just above her name. She had an old fashioned medical bag. She walked up to Nicole and very gently introduced herself, asking if she'd like Derek to go or stay. Nicole didn't want Derek out of her sight, so she asked him to stay.

"Always, love." He kissed her cheek. "Now let's get you checked out." He moved over and sat on the coffee table to make room for the doctor.

"I'm sorry to have to ask you this," the doctor said, "but did he sexually assault you as well?"

Tears streamed down Nicole's face as she shook her head, "No, Derek got there in time." She looked over at him, so immensely grateful.

"Ok, I'll examine your face, check your vitals, and examine your ribs to make sure nothing is broken." The doctor reached for her face. "I can also give you something for the pain and to calm your nerves."

"Thank you," was all that Nicole could say and she quietly let the doctor do her job.

As the doctor was feeling her ribs, she saw a man walk into the apartment carrying her own suitcase and purse. He went straight to the bedroom, opened up the closet, and started to unpack her things. Next, Victor arrived with a piece of paper, which he set on the kitchen counter. After Nicole assured Derek that she would be okay, he went to speak with both men in the bedroom.

Luckily, nothing was broken. The doctor told her that she would have a pretty bad headache from the bump on her head, but her eye would most likely not turn black and blue. Nicole tried her best to muster up a smile; only a woman would understand the vanity issues of having a black eye. The doctor told her that the force mostly hit her cheek bone and that might be sore for a few days. Nicole took the pills that she gave her, told her thank you, closed her eyes, and curled back up on the couch.

She could hear the sounds of a heated discussion between the three men. They weren't fighting but tempers were flaring. Nicole wanted to know who her attacker was. Was he there because of Derek? Was Derek's business really as legitimate as he had explained? What did she get herself wrapped up in? All of the questioning only made her head hurt more. She took a deep breath and reminded herself that Derek had saved her. But what if this happened again?

She heard all three men walk back into the room. Opening her eyes, she saw Derek letting the other two out.

"Was that Gael?" she asked quietly.

"Yes, and the other was Victor from across the street."

"Why did he have my things?"

"I didn't want you to have to go back into that hotel room again." he walked up to her. "Please stay here with me so I can protect you."

"Derek, what is going on?" She needed to understand what she needed protecting from. "Is this going to happen again?"

CHAPTER FOURTEEN

Derek closed the door behind Victor and Gael and turned to look at Nicole, curled up on the couch. It didn't seem real. It felt a little like his fighting days, when he would separate himself from what was happening to keep from changing the type of man he was inside. That type of fighting could not be personal or it would eat you alive.

He trusted Gael to handle the situation with the attacker so that he could focus solely on the beautiful woman in his living room. He could not believe this had happened to her. Could Silvia really be that crazy? He would make sure that she paid if she had caused one ounce of pain for Nicole. And rape? How could a woman wish that on another? Did Silvia really tell that man to rape Nicole? He was so glad the man hadn't been waiting in her room; he may not have heard her calls for help. The thought made his blood boil. He had never wanted to cause someone so much pain until now. He knew he had been close to killing him and in the moment, he didn't care.

Nicole wanted to know what was going on.

"I have a feeling I know who he is," he said to her, "And...he attacked you because of me."

She lifted her head and looked at him, anger in her eyes, "What?"

"I tried dating a local a few months back. She's a manager at Playa Vallarta." He stopped and waited for a response, but she stayed eerily still. He continued, "She confronted me when I was leaving the hotel the other morning and was crazy jealous I stayed the night with you. Then she sent a text last night when she heard about us leaving together. That has been the extent of it. I told her that if she confronted you in any way, I would have her fired." He waited again, but still nothing. He could tell Nicole wanted to hear everything before she reacted. "She told me once that if I get a tattoo here in Vallarta that I should use her cousin's artist. He had done an Aztec feather on the cousin's bicep."

Her eyes filled with tears as she rolled them back. "Okay, so you're not in some kind of mafia or a super-secret spy?"

"No, love, I just dated a woman that is apparently sadistic." He pulled her toward him. She took a couple of deep breaths, like she felt a little better about the entire situation. "He is going somewhere where he'll never be heard from again and she will be handled as well. I will make sure that if she is responsible for orchestrating this, she will pay dearly."

"Thank you," Nicole said, "and thank you for having my things brought here. I don't think I could ever go into that hotel room again."

"Can I take you away for a few days?" he asked her.

"Derek, I'm already on vacation. You don't take a vacation while on vacation." She said it sarcastically but still had tears in her eyes.

He laughed at her response. "This vacation seems like it could use at least a night away."

"Where would we go?"

"Nowhere far. We won't need a plane." He stood them both up. "My first investment property is in Nuevo Vallarta, just north of here. Come see my apartment there."

She looked like she was considering the idea.

"We won't pack a thing." He kissed her. "I can have it stocked with things from the shops nearby. I'll help you get cleaned up in the shower and Hector can drive us."

She didn't answer but started walking toward the bathroom, so he took that as a yes. He grabbed his phone on the way and told Hector to be outside with the car in half an hour.

In the bathroom, he turned on the shower so it could get hot and fill up with steam. He slowly undressed Nicole. There was nothing sexual about it. Though her body would always turn him on, he knew this was not the moment. This was about Nicole feeling safe, about her not having to think about anything. He was prepared for the fact that she may not even want to have sex for a while. Luckily, the man hadn't been able to violate her in that way, but that didn't take away from her experience. He wasn't sure how affected she would be. If she needed, he'd have Gael track down the best therapist in the area to talk to her.

He took Nicole's clothes into the bedroom. When he returned, he saw her standing, naked, looking at herself in the mirror as it slowly covered with steam. She touched the bump on her head and inspected the side of her cheek bone. He hoped that she knew how beautiful she looked, regardless of a bump and bruise. He also hoped they healed quickly so there wasn't the reminder looking back at her in the mirror.

The shower had a large glass wall. When he saw that it was full of steam, he took her hand and walked her into the shower. There was a big seat built into one of the walls. He asked if she'd like to sit down. Without a word, she did. He took the soap and washed her body. When he reached her face, he was careful not to hurt anywhere that was tender. He had never taken care of someone like this before. He took her hand and walked her over to the shower heads that sprayed from all directions. He washed and conditioned her hair for her. When they were finished, he grabbed a huge towel and wrapped it around her like she was an infant.

When they reached the bed, she took a deep breath and looked at him. "Thank you. That is what I needed. I needed you to wash all of that away. I don't want this to define me or us. I want it to be over. Can we do that?"

"Of course we can. Nicole, you tell me what you need and we will do it." He rarely used her name. He always used his pet name for her.

"I want you to take me to your apartment in Nuevo Vallarta. I want you to make me feel like my old self again. I want you to make love to me there."

"Hector will be outside in about ten minutes," he said to her.

"First, I need to call Kate. I'm not sure yet what I'll say but I need to call her." She looked confused and he felt sorry for her. He handed her the phone from his apartment. She dialed the number and waited.

"Hi, babe, it's me. I'm calling from Derek's," she said, wiping away silent tears. "Everything is fine, why?" It was so hard for him to listen to half of a conversation, especially one like this. "Derek is great. It got a little scary with one of his crazy ex-girlfriends but he's taking care of me." She listened. "No, still no word." Derek knew immediately that had to be the Maybe Boyfriend. He was relieved to hear that he hadn't tried to contact her. That was a good sign for him. "We're going up the coast to Nuevo Vallarta for the night." She listened again. "He has a place there as well... Yes, very lucky."

He decided that he should give her a little privacy. He wasn't sure why he had listened for so long already. He grabbed his cellphone and walked into the living room. First, he called the Samba Vallarta and let them know he'd be arriving and most likely only staying for the night. He also asked for the concierge to go to the shops and pick out plenty of options for Nicole. He already had everything there for himself.

Next, he dialed Gael's number and waited anxiously for him to answer. He was going to track down Silvia. Victor could handle the police with the attacker, which was rather straight forward. He was clearly guilty. It was Silvia's day off, which was most likely not a coincidence. If she had heard about her cousin being apprehended, she might be hiding. He needed someone with Gael's background to find her. She was not getting away with this. What were the chances of there being a random attack at Playa Vallarta, a perfectly safe hotel in a safe city, by another person that had the same tattoo as her cousin? Yes, Gael would find Silvia and he would deal with her.

By the time Gael answered, Derek was pacing the floor. "She has left her apartment," was how Gael answered the phone. "I found her passport, so she hasn't fled Mexico."

"Find her." Derek tried to keep his voice down. "I want her arrested with that piece of shit."

"I will find her before you return," Gael told him, before they ended the call.

Walking back into the bedroom, he saw that Nicole was off of the phone. She seemed a bit uneasy, like she wasn't sure she was the same person. That worried him a bit. When he heard her scream his name, something had happened inside of him. If there had ever been a wonder in his mind if Nicole was the one for him, it had vanished immediately in that moment. What Silvia had done completely backfired on her. Maybe she didn't know the route that her cousin was planning on taking, maybe she wanted him to scare Nicole into leaving her vacation and going home. It was a gamble with Nicole's life that Silvia should not have taken. All it did was make Derek one hundred percent sure that he was completely in love with Nicole. He wanted her with him always. He had been scared to trust his feelings about her so early in a relationship, but this had catapulted his emotions into overdrive and he trusted them now.

He knew he shouldn't talk to her about this yet. She knew he was there for her and that was enough. Right now, she needed to have a day or two away from everything to get back to feeling like herself and he was going to make sure that happened.

She put on one of the dresses he had bought her on their first day shopping- white with swirls of purple, blue, and pink. She pushed her sunglasses on her head to hold her wet hair away from her face. He loved how beautiful she looked in the dress. She was perfect for him and he hoped that she would discover the same thing regarding him.

They walked down to the street to where Hector was waiting with the running car. All of the madness from earlier was gone. It had turned back into a little street in a sleepy Mexican town. Derek opened the door for Nicole and asked her if she was ready.

"Let's get out of here." She mustered a smile, put on her sunglasses, and got into the car.

CHAPTER FIFTEEN

The drive up the coast did Nicole some good. She was really starting to feel better about the whole thing. However, it was a bit of a reality check. It's human nature to feel somewhat invincible. To feel that nothing would really ever happen to you. Those kinds of things happen to other people, to people you read about in newspapers. Well, she knew first hand now that those kinds of things could happen to her.

They pulled up to the hotel. It was bright and cheery, with white walls and a Spanish style roof. The bellman that opened the car door for them seemed to recognize Derek immediately. Hector got out of the car, said hello to some of the staff and a few words to Derek.

This still didn't seem real. She tried to imagine what it would be like to live on a resort all the time. It reminded her of a TV show that her father used to watch. She was pretty sure it was called *Hotel*, all about the staff of a hotel living on the property. It had seemed like such a strange concept to her as a kid. Now here she was, kind-of-dating a man that did just that.

Derek took Nicole's hand and led her through the lobby. They didn't need to check in, but he did go by and greet the people behind the counter. She noticed a few looks among them when he introduced her. She hadn't really considered the fact that maybe he didn't take women to *any* of his apartments; she had only been thinking about the Paraíso at the time. That led to her next question. How many apartments did he have? He said last night that he lived in "a lot" of places. "A lot" could mean anything.

She looked around the hotel. It had a quaint boutique atmosphere and was about the same size as all the other places they had passed. There was a cute little bar covered in Spanish tiles, one side facing the inside of the lobby and the other side facing the pool area. She hoped they stopped there for a drink tonight. She wondered what she'd wear. It was a little strange to think that there would be clothes in the closet that she didn't pick. Would they even fit?

In the elevator, he looked at her in a way he never had before, like he wasn't sure if she'd fall apart or not.

"Derek, I'm not going to break," she told him, not wanting it to be awkward. She hated what happened but she didn't want to let it ruin her time with him.

"I don't know if I would survive it if you had." His eyes were so sincere.

"We let her win if this comes between us. Her plan will have worked." She stood right in front of him and put her hands on his chest. "That thought is what's keeping me strong."

"You are a smart woman, love." He hesitated, but then leaned over and kissed her lightly on the lips, sweet and innocent. She wondered if he was going to make love to her when they reached the hotel room. She figured she needed to take matters into her own hands. They both needed sex to be a good thing and not the negative experience that had almost happened. In the past, she had always been a bit timid when it came to taking the lead. Nicole realized she may need to be a bit more forward than she was used to, to dig deep and be the initiator.

She stopped him before he opened the door to his room and asked, "Have you had a woman in here?"

"No, I've never brought a woman to any of these locations," he smiled at her.

"So that's why the staff had those looks on their faces when you introduced me."

"You caught that, huh? They'll be talking about this for days," he joked.

It was now or never for Nicole. She decided to play the dominant as best she could.

"Allow me," she said, motioning for the key.

"Welcome home, love," he said, smiling and handed it to her.

She opened the door and walked in. The room wasn't nearly as modern as the Paraíso apartment, but then again, this had been his first property. It looked like a suite that other guests might have in the hotel. There was a small kitchenette with a breakfast bar and two stools. The living room had wicker chairs, a dark blue couch with a coffee table and small TV stand with a slightly outdated television. Sliding glass doors led to a balcony with a table big enough for two people to comfortably sit. She wandered into the bedroom, which seemed like a basic hotel room except with far nicer bedding. The bathroom was clean, but what you would expect for a hotel. This place wasn't as fancy as the Paraíso, but she absolutely loved how drastically different it was. She wondered if all of Derek's places had their own style. What a fun way to live, the scenery always changing.

"How many apartments do you have?" she asked.

"Currently," he paused a moment before he answered, "I have 27 apartments at my disposal. But I spend most of my time in four of them. I only make quick visits to the others. Do you want to take some trips with me and see them all?"

She took a deep breath. "I'd love to. But first…" She walked up to him, closing her eyes because she was rather embarrassed. "Undress me."

She opened her eyes. Derek looked a bit caught off guard, still unsure if she would want to do this. She didn't take it personally; he had made it quite clear how much he desired her. She knew it was because of that morning. And she meant what she said. She wasn't going to let this little bitch win.

"What did I tell you, darlin'?" she smiled, "I'm not going to break. Undress me."

He smiled and slowly did what she said. He pushed each strap of her dress off of her shoulders until it fell to the floor. She looked down at herself and back up to him with an eyebrow raised. She didn't have to say a word for him to understand what she meant. He reached around and unhooked her lacy pink bra, then slid her matching panties over her hips until they fell to the floor with her dress.

"That's better," she said, "now do something about your clothes."

She couldn't believe how naturally this was coming to her. It was exhilarating and empowering. She watched him undress before walking him over to the bed and pushing him back until he fell onto it. Then she crawled on top of him, as sensually as she could.

"I want you to make me cum. I don't want you to stop until I call out your name. Can you do that for me?"

Without a word, he flipped himself on top of her and kissed her neck. She started laughing, unable to help herself. "Take that, Little Bitch." She had decided that would be her nickname for that woman.

"Exactly right," he told her, "Now let's work on that name calling."

It was hard and fast this time. Nicole had set the tone for it and she loved it. Her past experiences with boyfriends had always been one way or the other. With Andrew, it was always slower, never as passionate as with Derek, and definitely never even close to fucking. The bad boys of her younger past had, for the most part, only wanted it fast. If she tried to slow it down for a change of pace, they never took her cues. And she hadn't been comfortable enough to talk about it with them either.

Now she was sprawled on top of Derek, trying to catch her breath. He had a firm grip around her still. She loved how worried he was for her, but she hoped that he would get past it. He must have known what she was thinking because he said, "I will be okay once Gael finds Silvia. Once I know she's arrested, I will put my guard down."

"That's her name? I like Little Bitch better, personally."

"Yes, it suits her." He kissed her head as a silent thank you that she seemed to understand.

After the day's excitement and their adventure in the bedroom, they wandered in and out of a sleepy haze for the rest of the day. It was exactly what they both needed: an entire twenty-four hours of sleep to recharge their batteries. They stayed curled up under the blankets, enjoying the time together, laughing and talking.

When they finally decided to be part of the land of the living again, he asked, "Are you hungry?"

"I'm famished!" she said, getting out of bed and stretching her muscles.

"Take a look in the closet. I told them to get you some options. There should be dresses, pants, tops, bathing suits, running stuff, lingerie, anything you need. I figured we could leave them for next time..." He let that last part trail off as he walked into the living room. She smiled at that thought. Oh Lord, she needed to do something about Andrew.

She ran through the shower and picked out a strapless linen dress in coral that somehow fit her perfectly. While Derek was getting ready, she walked out onto the balcony to check out the view. She leaned against the railing, looking at the people below on the beach, and wondered when she was going to wake up from this dream. It still didn't seem quite real that she was here.

She could see the edge of the pool and part of the bar. In between, there was one of those oversized chess boards where each person would have to lug the pieces around in between moves. She loved chess. She admittedly hadn't played in years, but thought that it must be like riding a bike.

Just at that moment, Derek came up and put his arms on either side of her, grabbing the railing around her to lean in close. He kissed the back of her neck and they stood there watching the view together.

"Wanna play chess?" she asked him.

"Sure. I warn you that I'm pretty good," he teased.

"It's been awhile since I've played, but I'll put up a good fight," she turned around to face him and kissed his lips.

"Let's go before we never leave this room." He grabbed her hand and they walked back inside. "I love that dress on you. I'll have to ask Maria where she bought it and we'll do some more shopping."

Normally she would fight him on that idea, but she was beginning to realize that a shopping spree probably wouldn't put a dent in his wallet. She grabbed her little purse and they headed for the lobby. The huge chess board was set up close to some tables. They settled down in one of them and a waiter came over to bring some menus. He knew Derek and after they said their hellos, he introduced her again as *"Mi Amor*, Nicole." She loved hearing him say that.

They ordered a variety of appetizers to munch on while they played. As they waited for their drinks Nicole looked around. The hotel was beautiful. There were palm trees everywhere and an enormous pool wound all around the large patio. Everywhere she looked, there was a different section. She saw a kid's area that had the feel of a splash pad and large waterfalls with coves underneath for couples to steal kisses. There was a swim-up bar with groups of people on barstools, laughing and taking shots while they splashed in the water. Her favorite part may have been the bar along the patio with swings attached at the overhang that served as bar seats. She definitely wanted to try those out.

Their drinks arrived. Derek stuck with a beer while she had a house cocktail that was a mixture of different liquors and juices in a glass big enough to be a fishbowl. He laughed at her attempts to pick it up and take a drink. Eventually, she opted to lean over and leave it right where the waiter had set it on the table.

They each chose a side on the oversized chess board. It never occurred to Nicole that seeing the entire board from above was a much better vantage point for the game. She realized it was much harder to play from such a different angle and she began to worry about her abilities. Luckily, she moved her first pawn and realized they were much lighter than expected. The pawns came up to about her knees and the larger pieces reached her thighs. Of course, Derek was a shrewd chess player; he knew how to assemble his players to keep her from advancing at all. Rather quickly, it became clear that her only chance was to play defense.

They laughed and talked while they played, enjoying the appetizers between turns. The waiter had brought out some quesadillas, little fish tacos, stuffed jalapenos, and chips with salsa and guacamole. Everything tasted marvelous. She suggested they go for a run on the beach in the morning after all of the fabulous food. At some point, Derek's phone rang and she could tell by the look on his face that it had to be Gael. They both sat down at the table and he held her hand while he answered.

Nicole tried not to eavesdrop on the short conversation, even though it did concern her. She knew that he'd fill her in afterwards. Smiling at him, she stood up to walk over to get a better view of the beach, where the hotel staff were setting up for a wedding. She smiled, thinking about her writing. Back in college, she never would have thought that she'd be writing for a local magazine in the bridal section. But it turned out that she loved writing about weddings. As she watched them set up the altar and the chairs on the sand, she wondered what she would write about this one.

There was a little woman adjusting all of the bows tied to the back of the chairs and a tall, thin man that was arranging the flowers along the altar. She wondered who was getting married and what their love story was. Nicole always interviewed the bride and groom along with some of the wedding party to get a better feel for the couple. She could tell immediately if there was an overbearing mother of the bride or if the families didn't get along. Of course those were never mentioned in her stories. With all the drama of wedding planning, they should always be looked back upon with wonderful memories. She remembered learning that weddings are never perfect, but it could be considered a perfect wedding if the bride and guests were never aware of the issues.

She wasn't sure how long she had been watching the scene set below her when she felt Derek's arms curl around her waist. She leaned her head back against his chest. After only a week, she already knew his smell and the feeling of his body.

"What did he say?" she asked blankly.

"Gael was able to interview the man. It was Silvia's cousin. He gave them any information possible to try and stay out of jail. I will make sure that doesn't happen," he said and kissed her head.

"What did he tell Gael?"

"She worked the night shift the other night and when she figured we weren't coming back to your room, she realized that I took you to my place. She never liked that I wouldn't take her there." He took a deep breath. "So she called her cousin and paid him to wait for you. He told Gael that she said to 'scare you and rough you up a little bit.' He obviously thought he'd take it a step further." He felt her head where it had hit the wall. "It's still swollen a bit. Does it hurt?"

"A little but it will heal," she touched the side of her face when she spoke. "This is tender."

He turned her toward him and kissed it very lightly. "I will make sure he doesn't get off for this. I don't know if he's done this before, but I'm worried he has a taste for it now. Gael said that she was most likely hiding at her friend's house. He is going to continue tracking her down." He saw that she had been watching the set up for the wedding. "The Samba does quite a few weddings, two or three a month." She looked up and saw that he had a concentrated look on his face. Like he was trying to see specific details below that he couldn't quite get into focus.

"Maybe we'll have a beach wedding one day," he said, almost as if he wasn't talking to her, but rather accidentally said it out loud what was in his head. She didn't respond, just squeezed him tight.

CHAPTER SIXTEEN

Did he say that thing about their beach wedding out loud? He was pretty sure that he had but Nicole didn't say anything. He silently prayed to God that he hadn't. He wanted to think for a bit and he wanted Nicole to be able to relax.

"I scheduled you a massage," he said to her and kissed her head again.

She turned around to look at him. "But you haven't completely annihilated me in chess yet," she smiled, "A massage sounds fabulous right now though."

"Perfect. I'll show you the spa. Get whatever you'd like. You should become very familiar with the place. It'll be their job from now on to pamper you whenever you'd like it."

"Do you enjoy spoiling me?" she teased him.

"It's becoming one of my favorite things." With one last kiss, he took her hand and they wandered toward the spa.

He was hesitant to let her out of his sight. Luckily, he hadn't dated any of the women in the spa so that made him feel better. A tall, slender woman named Irma took Nicole back for her massage, assuring Derek that she would be in good hands. The spa was the one place that he was not familiar with. Since he never brought women to his hotels, he hadn't had a reason to visit the area. He preferred to run for relaxation, he never got into massages for himself.

Derek paced the hallway outside of the spa for the first ten minutes or so. He wanted to have his eyes on Nicole or at least know that no suspicious-looking person was wandering into the area. But he needed to get a grip, so he decided to schedule their dinner for the night. The hotel usually only had beachside candlelight dinners on the weekends, but he thought they may make an exception for him. He called and talked with the manager and got everything set.

Ultimately, Derek wanted Nicole to live like he did, on the hotel properties with him. He knew that wasn't fair for him to ask for that, especially this early on. However, he was ready to talk with her about the Maybe Boyfriend. Something had to be done about him. This relationship was getting far too serious, he hoped on both sides, to have someone waiting at home. From what he could gather, Maybe Boyfriend hadn't tried to contact her. Maybe that meant they were already broken up in his head, but maybe wasn't good enough. A man would be crazy to want to break things off with a woman like Nicole.

It took everything in him not to call Gael again and ask for an update on the Silvia situation. The woman was causing all kinds of problems. Derek knew that Gael should be focused on the Chicago deal for their client and instead he was tracking down this Little Bitch. (He laughed, remembering Nicole's name for her.) What new developments could have arisen in the past hour or so? What if he couldn't find her today? Should they stay in Nuevo Vallarta? He needed to come up with a plan to keep Nicole safe.

This Chicago deal was Gael's thing but Derek would still get an apartment out of it. If it weren't for Nicole, he may not ever visit the location. He really had had no urge to return to the States before. Now, he thought he might spend a good amount of time there.

For now, one idea would be to take her to Cancun if he needed to give Gael a few days to track Silvia down. He wasn't ready to take Nicole back to the Paraíso with Silvia still out there. If the hotel company in Cancun ended up choosing Chicago to expand, he thought Nicole should see the type of property where she'd hopefully spend a lot of their time when he was up there.

She already lived and worked downtown and he hoped that she was planning on moving out on her own. Ideally, the property would be up and running rather quickly and she could live there indefinitely. He'd rent her a condo in the nicest building until it was ready. He wasn't sure she'd accept the offer, but he'd figure out a way to make it happen. He would love for her to travel with him until the Chicago location was open, but he knew she'd worry about her job. Maybe she could take a leave of absence?

Another thought had crossed his mind while watching the setup for the wedding with Nicole. He wanted to discuss the idea with Gael first. He needed someone to tell him if he'd lost his mind before he brought it up to her. For now, he knew it was only fair to only ask for small changes in her life.

He sat down in a chair in the hallway and decided to open his emails on his phone. He was normally more focused on work than he had been in the past week. It dawned on him that maybe he went looking for work every day to fill the time. He had set everything up so that his money worked for him now. With very few living expenses, his personal wealth grew with each year. He was thinking about all twenty-seven locations that Stone Hospitality had helped acquire and running through rough calculations in his head. Most of his apartments could be rented as either suites or super suites. If he put those back into rotation at most of the properties, that would bring in quite a bit of revenue.

Derek couldn't believe how much he was ready to change his lifestyle. He had always requested that his apartments not be rented when he wasn't there. He had personal items in each one so that he never had to travel with a suitcase, which didn't allow for the space to be rented while he was away. He wondered if he should keep a handful at his disposal. If he wanted to travel to any of the properties with Nicole in the future, then he could technically "rent" them as other guests did. It would bring in far more revenue for those companies and he did get a small percentage of that revenue.

Once this Silvia thing was figured out, he wanted to schedule a meeting with Gael to talk about his interest in Derek's ideas for the company. Derek didn't want to assume that Gael would like a larger role than he had now. Maybe he would like some of the property apartments as well. There was a lot to figure out and decide.

Finally, Nicole walked out of the spa, looking relaxed beyond belief. Her long, wavy hair was slicked back from the oils used to massage her head. She came up and sat down on his lap, throwing her arms around his neck.

"Thank you," she smiled at him, "That was so relaxing."

"You can get a massage any time you'd like one," he told her sincerely, "I made us reservations on the beach for dinner. What would you like to do before then? We have a few hours."

"Let's sit on those swings by the bar. I've always loved swings!"

He lifted her from his lap and they walked out to the lobby of the hotel. There were a few guests sitting on the lobby side of the bar and most of the bar seats were full on the pool side. Luckily, the swings were open. Nicole ran over and hopped on one like a little girl. She looked at him with a huge smile and pushed herself off of the side of the bar so that she could swing back. "This is awesome!" she laughed.

He smiled while he watched her. He lightly pushed his feet off and let his body weight bring the swing back to the bar. He had never sat in the swings before and found they were pretty fun. Nicole was bringing out a playful side in him. He ordered them each a soda. He wasn't sure if this was the exact time to bring up the Maybe Boyfriend, but seemed as good a time as any. He knew he was going to sound a little crazy and was probably going to sound even crazier than he thought. Still, he couldn't help himself. Once this was figured out, hopefully they could enjoy their dinner on the beach with some kind of long-distance commitment between the two of them.

"Now that I have you relaxed and happy, can we discuss something?"

"Did you hear from Gael?" she said with a worried sound in her voice.

"No, love, nothing like that." He hesitated for a moment. "I'd like to talk to you about the situation with the Maybe Boyfriend at home."

"I've done a lot of thinking about that," she said. He liked that she had already thought about it. And, he hoped that since they were here in Nuevo Vallarta together, that she had chosen him and not the Maybe Boyfriend.

"Did you come to any decisions? Because I don't think I can handle knowing you're going home to this Maybe Boyfriend. I know I sound insane but you're worth that risk." He waited for her answer with baited breath, trying to keep a calm composure.

She smiled at him sweetly. "This trip has made me discover that Andrew, that's his name by the way, is not the right person for me."

Honestly, he hated even knowing his name. He didn't like thinking of anything that made him seem more like a real person. And now he had a name. Derek was annoying himself with his reaction; what the hell was she going to think? "That is a relief." He tried to relax his body just a bit. He knew himself well enough to know that they were going to need to talk more about this. Nicole must have men hitting on her every day. If she went home a single woman, she'd quickly end up on a date or with another boyfriend. He wasn't kidding when he said he couldn't handle it. He wasn't sure how to tell her everything he was thinking.

"Were you planning on telling him when you got home?" He tested the waters.

"I hadn't thought of when I'd tell him," she admitted.

He was searching his brain for a suave way of handling this, but ultimately, he knew that he would fall short. *What the hell*, he thought to himself and continued, "Will you hear me out about some things?" He waited for her to reply.

"Of course."

"I hope that this thing between us seems as serious to you as it does to me. As you can tell, I am somewhat of a protective and jealous man. I don't want you waiting until you're home to tell him. I'd love for you to tell him now so that we can spend the rest of your time together without him hanging in the background. I want you to go home in a committed relationship with me. Somehow, we'll make this work. Nicole, I know that I am in love with you." When he finished, he took a deep breath and tried to figure out what she was thinking. Nicole had a pretty good poker face. Was she getting nervous about his jealousy issues?

"Derek, I love you too. I know this is fast, but it feels like love." She smiled and pushed herself back and forth on the swing a few times. He didn't respond yet; she seemed to have more to say. "Hmmmm, tell him over the phone?"

"Yes," he stated simply.

"That seems kind of rude, after three years, not to tell him in person." He wasn't sure if she was asking him to change his mind. He couldn't help himself. Crazy or not, he wasn't going to.

"Yes, normally I would agree. But, after three years, he knew you were getting on the plane and didn't care where you were going," he pointed out.

She looked like she was considering that point, "That is true."

"Has he tried to contact you at all since you've been here?" He figured at this point he shouldn't be worried about overstepping his bounds.

"He left me one message the second or third night I was here. He said that he had avoided calls from Kate when she was worried and he asked if I was ready to tell him where I was." The fact that she heard his voice, even on a message, drove him nuts. He realized his fists were clenched and he had ripped up the napkin that was in front of him. Good lord, he was losing it. He could tell she noticed his reaction. "What is it?" She didn't sound mad, more confused.

"So he didn't know where you were going. I can't describe it completely; I don't like the idea of you talking to him at all. I already think of you as my girlfriend, not his." He tried to relax his hands "If you'd let me, I'll hire a moving company and get you a condo so that you can go straight home to a new place. Any chance you'd take me up on that?"

"Derek, I love you. But I'm not comfortable living somewhere I haven't seen," she said, "That's too weird for me."

"Where will you go when you get back?" he asked seriously.

"I'm sure I can stay with Kate till I find a place. I don't think friends should live together long term but she'd put me up for a few weeks." She was trying to make him feel better, but it wasn't helping.

"Will you please call him and break it off here? I know I sound a bit psychotic, but after this morning I don't like that I won't be there to protect you if he gets mad." He was serious.

"He wouldn't do something like that Derek." Was she defending him now?

"You don't know that for sure. I would have never thought Silvia would do that either." He honestly never thought she would have. He wasn't prepared to now trust this man he'd never met. "Nicole, this is important to me. I would like to have dinner with you tonight as my girlfriend. I would like to make love to you tonight in our bed with no one thinking you're coming back to them in Chicago."

Something was going through that gorgeous head and he couldn't figure out what. Without another thought, he pulled her off of her swing and sat her on his lap. He put his forehead against hers and closed his eyes. He loved the way she smelled. He kissed her gently and he didn't care if he sounded like he was begging as he asked again, "Please."

"How could I say no to that?" She kissed him again. He was so relieved. He let out a huge breath that he didn't know he had been holding in.

CHAPTER SEVENTEEN

As they walked back to the room, Nicole couldn't believe she was about to make the phone call. Overall, she was not good with confrontation, so maybe the nudge was a good thing. If she had to tell Andrew when she got home, then she may have put off the inevitable for too long. And that wouldn't be fair to anyone.

She wasn't exactly sure what she was going to say. Was she going to tell him about Derek or leave him out of it? She felt sick to her stomach. She wanted to call Kate first. Kate could always calm her down and remind her of what she needed to do.

She walked into Derek's apartment and went to sit on the couch, trying not to look worried. She didn't want him to misread her emotions. She really wasn't scared for it to be over with Andrew, but she was scared to tell Andrew that. Derek walked over to her and knelt on the floor in front of her so that they were almost eye to eye with each other.

"Do you want this? Do you want me?" Even when he was in a very vulnerable state, he still looked tough. That made him even sexier. Somehow he pulled off both at the same time and it made her want to drag him into the bedroom… Oh, this man.

"I really do Derek. I don't like confrontation, is all." She rested her arms on his shoulders and this time she put her forehead against his. "I've never had a long distance relationship before, but we'll figure it out."

He kissed her and put her phone in her hand. "I'm going to give you some privacy. I won't be far."

"Thank you. I may call Kate first, so give me some time." She tried to smile, but her nerves had taken over again. He kissed her cheek and left the apartment.

When she turned on her phone, she realized that maybe Andrew would have tried to reach her again. It would be harder if he had. When her phone came to life, she had two text message and no voicemails. The first was from Kate, telling her that she wanted to hear all about the ex-girlfriend when they talked again.

The second was from Andrew. All it read was, "Where are you?" That was it. There was no apology, no please, not even a phone call. Was he worried? Was he annoyed? She couldn't tell anything from those three stupid words. One thing she knew was that she was now annoyed.

She dialed Kate's number. It was a Thursday afternoon; Kate would be at work. She was a divorce attorney, of all things. That was how Nicole had met Andrew originally, through Kate's circle of lawyer friends. As long as she wasn't with a client or in court, Kate would answer the phone.

Kate picked up quickly with, "Nic, how are you?"

"Hi," Nicole responded, "this hotel is fabulous as well. I'll tell you all about the ex-girlfriend fiasco another time. I want your advice."

"Sure, honey," was all Kate said.

"I need to call Andrew and break it off. Derek doesn't want me to wait till I'm home. Is that bad?" Her voice practically cracked as it went up an octave.

"Oh lord, I guess it depends on if you want to break it off or if he's pressuring you?"

"I do want to break it off," she told her, "You know me; I don't like confrontation. I probably wouldn't do it over the phone, but maybe I need the push to do it at all."

"That's a good point. Nic, I see more emotions and fight in the people I represent getting divorced. If there hasn't been that level of emotion with you and Andrew in three years, I'm not sure it'll come. As long as this is what you want to do, I don't think he's wrong to ask for it now. You're sleeping with him, right? Would you want him to have a girlfriend waiting at home?"

"God, no I wouldn't. Thank you, that's what I needed to hear. Love you and we'll talk tomorrow."

"Love you, too." And she was gone. Nicole sat there staring at her phone in her hand. What was she going to say? She leaned her head back on the couch and closed her eyes. She didn't want to see Derek's apartment while she was talking to Andrew. She opened her eyes long enough to call Andrew and closed them quickly again.

"Hello, Stranger." Andrew's voice sounded normal. Not worried, not relieved, not even mad. She got more emotions from her friend than from her "boyfriend." His tone empowered her a bit.

"Hey, we need to talk," was all she could think to say.

"Where are you?"

"Kate knew."

"So, you've talked to Kate but not me." Now he started sounding annoyed.

"Yes, pretty much," she snapped back.

"I don't remember all of the God damned places that your father traveled. He was all over the globe, Nicole. Where are you?!" She didn't like how he was ordering her to tell him. He must have realized how he sounded because she heard a deep breath on the other end of the phone and he continued, "Nicole, I love you. When are you coming home?" Ugh, that made it a little harder, hearing him refer to their home together. Still, she was determined to do this. She couldn't face Derek and tell him she didn't have the guts to end it.

"I'm in Puerto Vallarta, Dad's heaven on Earth, remember?" She paused, but he didn't answer, so she continued, "Andrew, you left without knowing where I was going. You stayed gone until I had to leave for the airport. That speaks volumes to me. It's been three years and we're not moving forward. I'm okay with that because I don't think we're supposed to." She took the deep breath this time. "I'm going to stay with Kate for a while when I get back. This isn't going to work with us anymore."

"Your dad just died. You're not thinking clearly."

"Exactly, Andrew, my dad just died and you let me board a plane alone. You didn't want to inconvenience your life enough to come with me and give me support."

"I will come this weekend," Andrew replied, "I have a meeting tomorrow, but I'll book a flight for just after that. I can get there tomorrow night. What hotel are you in?"

Oh no, she was going to have to tell him about Derek. She had hoped to keep him out of it. She wasn't about to tell him where she was staying. They already had to deal with the Little Bitch and she hadn't even been found yet. She didn't want to add to their drama. "There isn't any point, Andrew."

"Yes, there is. I will make this up to you and show you how much I love you." It was a sweet gesture, but she had already seen his true colors. When it came down to it, she lost her father and he wasn't there for her.

"Don't come here. I met someone and he's been taking care of me in your absence." She knew it was a bitchy thing to say, but she just couldn't help herself. At first, she thought that she was mad that he didn't know where she was going. Maybe it was being with a man like Derek, but she wanted more concern and protection now. She craved that type of a man and Andrew wasn't one of them. Now she was even more angry that he hadn't come with her. She didn't want him here anymore. But she had known it was over since she had boarded the plane alone.

"What? Have you fucked him? You have, haven't you?" Andrew rarely swore. It was how she knew he was really mad, when he dropped the f-bomb. Again, he rethought his approach. "I'm sorry, Nicole, I shouldn't have said that. This guy is taking advantage of you in your emotional state. I will come and spend the rest of the trip with you. We will get through this."

"If he were taking advantage of me, *which he's not*, you weren't here to protect me from his advances!" She realized she was yelling. She hoped that Derek wasn't sitting outside of the door because he would have heard that for sure. At least he'd know that she was standing up for him. She was so angry, but the thought of Derek melted her heart in that moment. She didn't notice she had opened her eyes while she yelled. She closed them again and saw Derek's gorgeous eyes and strong face. She imagined his strong arms wrapped around her and her body felt his kisses all over her. That was love. This was not. "Andrew, it's over."

And she hung up the phone.

Thank God she hadn't told him where she was staying. Then again, she didn't think he really had it in him to come there knowing she was *fucking* another man. She wished she had told him that they had, in fact, fucked and they had also made love, with more passion that she ever had with Andrew. Nicole knew deep down that she hadn't said that to him because it would have been mean. She honestly didn't want to hurt him; she just wanted it to be over. She wanted to be free of that relationship so that she could focus on one with Derek.

Now that she could do that, she wondered how they would make this work. Could she be in a long-distance relationship? She couldn't imagine being away from him now, but maybe she would get used to it. Maybe they could take turns visiting each other. She'd love to see all of his different hotels. What a fun way to date.

Just then, she realized that she had told Andrew she'd be staying with Kate. She should probably ask her. She looked around for the phone and found it across the couch. She must have thrown it across the room when she hung up on Andrew. He hadn't tried to call back, not that she expected him to after these past few days. She dialed Kate again.

"Three times in one day. I'm a lucky girl," Kate joked when she answered the phone.

"Yes, you are my dear. And you're about to get even luckier. You're going to have a roommate until I can find an apartment," she joked back and then got serious before her friend could respond, "I did it, Kate. I broke it off. Could I stay with you for a few weeks? I promise I'll find somewhere fast, maybe somewhere in your building? How fun would that be?!"

"Of course you can. That would be fun. We wouldn't have to freeze our asses off in the winter to get to each other's places. Can I pick up some of your stuff for you?"

Damn it. "Ugh, I hadn't thought about that," Nicole admitted, "I really don't want to see him. I have my things from this trip. If you could help me grab some things while he's at work, I'd wait on the big stuff till I find a place." Things were actually coming together. "Derek did offer to get me a condo and have everything moved in before I get home. But that's too crazy."

"Holy shit, Nic, who is this guy?" She laughed when she said it but Nicole was pretty sure she was serious about the question.

"Remember I told you he was a UFC fighter way back when? Well apparently, he was pretty good. He invested his money and started this company and now he is involved in all these hotels everywhere. He lives in them, too. I think he's pretty rich, Kate. But he's like my dad. If you met him, you'd never guess."

"Wow. But I agree. Stay with me for a few weeks. Gotta get back to work, talk to you tomorrow." Nicole could hear her talking to someone in her office as she hung up the phone.

She had done it; everything was settled. She rummaged through the kitchen cabinets until she found the alcohol, contemplating what would be the appropriate celebratory drink. She settled on a bottle of fine bourbon. She liked the brand and figured this had to be a good bottle. It wasn't opened, but Derek wouldn't mind. He'd be proud of her for calling. She grabbed two glasses and filled them with ice and whisky, almost to the top. Balancing them in one hand, she opened the door and went searching for him.

Of course he hadn't gone far. She saw him before he even noticed she was out there. He was typing on his phone and she could tell he was concentrating. Silvia popped into her head, but her news was more important. She knew Derek would protect her from anything Silvia could throw at them. They would fight her together. Right now, she wanted to have a drink with her boyfriend. God, she liked the sound of that.

CHAPTER EIGHTEEN

Derek thought he heard Nicole yell at one point, but he was determined to let her handle it. She had agreed to call Andrew, so now he needed to give her the space to do it. And yelling was good. At least she wasn't talking dirty to him. The thought made him sick. In the past, he never particularly liked the idea of being the other man. But when he had known a woman was cheating on her boyfriend with him while on vacation, it never bothered him when she returned home to the man's bed.

Nicole was an entirely different story. He tried to focus on business to keep his mind off of the conversation. It wasn't working; he had read the same line in an email at least ten times. He strained his ears to listen and, knowing he'd do that, had sat far enough away to give her privacy. He hated thinking of her having any contact with Andrew, even if it was to break it off. He hated even knowing the man's name. He hated a lot of things in that moment.

Then relief came. He saw Nicole walking up to him with two rocks glasses full of ice and an amber liquid. He wondered which drink she had poured them. She had the sweetest smile on her face, which was a good sign for the outcome of her conversation. He closed down his email as soon as he saw her coming. Work could wait.

"A drink for my boyfriend," she said with a laugh.

"Did it go okay? Do you need any time to yourself?" He honestly wanted her to be happy with her decision.

"No, I don't want to be alone. He wasn't happy to hear about you, but then again, I don't blame him. You were serious competition." She winked and took a drink. "I opened that nice bottle of whisky in your cabinet. I hope you don't mind."

"*Our* cabinet and of course I don't mind. It was a nice choice." He took a drink of the glass she had handed him. It tasted wonderful, smooth going down. The smell and taste of this particular brand would always remind him of when Nicole was officially his. He wanted to keep a bottle of it stocked in his apartments from now on.

"So he heard about me?" he inquired. He wasn't sure she'd want to talk about this, but he was curious. He couldn't help asking.

"Yes, he offered to finally come. I told him he wasn't needed and that you were taking care of me in his absence."

"Nice response, love. Are you sure you don't need some time? Would you like to take a nap before dinner? We could cancel that as well."

"There's no need to cancel dinner. I've been broken up with him in my head almost as soon as we met. I just needed to officially tell him. I'm really fine but you're sweet to ask." She seemed like she was okay. "Want to take a walk on the beach?" she asked.

"That sounds great."

He stood up and took her hand. He loved this hotel. Given that it was his first one, it had always been very close to his heart. It had been the start of everything for him and here he was, starting all over with Nicole.

They reached the beach and aimlessly wandered in one direction. Derek took her shoes and his flip flops and hung them from the fingers of one hand, holding her hand in the other. They walked close enough so that the waves could reach up to their ankles. Nicole laughed at the shock of the cold water the first time it rushed towards them. It felt great to be there with her. Somehow, she made life feel complete for him.

He had never really felt love before. He never loved his mother and she never loved him. He felt a sense of responsibility for her now, as a successful man, but she had never taken care of him. After experiencing the level of his feelings for Nicole, he understood what love was supposed to be like. Derek was glad that he hadn't figured that out before this. If he had, it would have been harder to swallow. But now, it only made him that much more appreciative that Nicole was in his life.

There was always so much to talk about with her; he wasn't sure which topic to choose. He thought that filling her in on his ideas about Gael and the company was as good a topic as any. But then he looked at her and she was watching some children play in the sand. Maybe that was a better topic.

"Do you see yourself with kids in the future?" He had never thought about the subject too much, so he wasn't hoping for any particular answer. He was rather surprised that he'd be okay with whatever she answered.

"I would like at least one with the right person," she replied, "They haven't been on my radar, but I also know I'm not getting any younger. I'm thirty-three; it gets harder as you get older." She didn't take her eyes off the kids. A smile came over her face as she watched them. "I don't have any close friends with children yet.

Everyone is focusing on careers or still just getting married. Do you want them?"

"I've never thought about it, sadly. My lifestyle is not normal, which has made it hard to consider anything long term enough for children to be in the picture." Here they were: two people in love that had not thought much about family in the future. They had barely known each other for a week. Maybe he needed to let the subject go for now. That thought brought him right back to his ideas about Gael.

"I've been batting around the idea of letting Gael take on a larger role in the company." She looked up at him, but didn't answer. He explained a bit more, "I have always been a bit of a control freak with my company. I did the research, I chose the locations, and I only trusted myself. I was always looking for the next plot of land in the right area to keep myself busy. You can't lounge on the beach all the time," he smiled at her while she listened, "I do enjoy the work, but I've worked as much as I have to fill up my time. I can let my money work more for me now, if I choose to."

"You're very lucky you can do that. Does that mean you'll be able to visit me more?" she said slyly.

"It definitely does."

He still wanted her to stay with him and travel, but with her question about visiting Chicago, he didn't think she would be receptive to that yet.

"Any chance you'd agree to live on the Chicago property when it's up and running?" he asked, thinking that it was a good way of testing the waters.

"Oh wow, I don't know. If it was in downtown maybe I would." Her eyes brightened at the thought. "Is it going to happen for sure?"

"With Gael focusing on Silvia, I communicated with our client. He's extremely serious and he trusts my judgment on this since I've proven myself to them in the past. They have begun the first part of the negotiations. If all goes well, it could be open in six to nine months."

"My friends would be so jealous," she laughed again.

"Let's head back and get ready for dinner," he suggested.

Walking inside the apartment again with Nicole, with no Maybe Boyfriend, felt freeing. It was finally their place. He couldn't believe how much he liked thinking of his things as theirs. He had protected his personal life for so long and now he was ready to share everything with her. If she really did want to return to Chicago, he hoped that she would agree to live on the new property. He wondered if his desire had anything to do with being able to keep eyes on her.

It wasn't that he wanted to make sure there weren't men with her; he could trust her. It was a safety thing. He liked knowing that employees would have their eye on her. He would make sure everyone who worked there had extensive background checks. He didn't want to risk another incident with Nicole's life. Then again, there would have been no way to check for someone like Silvia. He wouldn't be dating any women in Chicago. Hopefully that would rule out the Silvia-type problem.

He must have looked deep in thought because Nicole walked up to him in the kitchen, wrapped her arms around his neck, and asked, "What is going on inside that handsome head?"

"I'm thinking about us. I love this." He nuzzled himself into her hair at the nape of her neck. "I could get used to having you around."

They showered, which he discovered was far more fun with Nicole than on his own. After an extra-long and enjoyable shower, she sat in front of their closet, looking at all of the choices. "Good lord, this woman can shop," she said, "These dresses are gorgeous." Derek simply smiled at her, fairly sure that she was talking to herself. He liked that she did that. It gave him little snippets of what was going through her mind.

She chose a bold yellow dress that was short but loosely fitted, with three-quarter length sleeves and wide slits in the shoulders. She paired it with some strappy black heels. She looked beautiful. He walked up behind her and whispered into her ear, "Check out the top drawer of the dresser. Maria picked up some jewelry for you."

She turned around and made a little audible squeal and opened the drawer. She chose a thick black necklace, a great contrast to the yellow in the dress. She looked beautiful and trendy. He grabbed a pair of pants and a casual plaid shirt with light, muted colors. When they were ready, they headed for the door.

In the elevator, Nicole noticed the music coming from a stage area where a band was playing. "After dinner, wanna do some shots and go dancing?" she asked, "I feel like getting drunk and celebrating."

"Absolutely, love." He liked the idea of seeing her dance and getting to be the man she danced with.

There was a single table sitting at the edge of the beach, a white table cloth blowing in the breeze. A candle burned on the table and tiki torches were set up for additional light. A bottle of Brut Private Cuvee arrived at the table. Derek loved a nice bottle of champagne and wanted this one to be a bit over the top. This was a huge night for them as a couple; he wanted it to be perfect. The fact that Nicole wanted to get drunk and dance only made it better. An elegant meal on the beach to start and then ending the night on the casual side was exactly what they needed.

While they enjoyed their dinner, Nicole asked more about where his other properties were located. He saw it as a good sign that she was interested in visiting them. He went through the list from start to finish, which included most of the vacation destination spots in Mexico, the Caribbean, and parts of Central and South America. He told her little bits about everything, from the quaint towns like Turks and Caicos to the hustle and bustle of areas like Rio.

They both opted to skip something sweet at the table and drink their dessert instead. They made their way towards the band playing on the stage outside. There was a bar full of people listening to the music close by. Derek kept a tight hold of Nicole's hand as he navigated his way to the one of the bartenders. He ordered them each a tequila flight with a selection of five types of tequila.

"If we're going to do this, let's do it right." He winked at her as they each picked up the first shot. He loved watching her drink. There was a party girl inside of her and he loved that she was all his. She licked the salt off the rim of the shot glass and threw her head back, a lime wedge waiting in her hand to offset the burn of the tequila. Her scrunched face was priceless, but she also looked like she enjoyed it.

"Another?" she said just as she finished the first. He was prepared to let her get as drunk as she needed tonight. He didn't envy the hangover she may have tomorrow, but he'd be there to take care of her. Soon after the second, she was ready for the third.

"Let's dance," he suggested. After all, they'd split a bottle of champagne and taken three shots of tequila. He wanted her to have fun, not black out. He took her to the dance floor and pulled her close to him. The band was playing a salsa that allowed them to dance close. The alcohol had gone to his head and he could see that it had with her as well. Her eyes were a bit glazed over and she had a dreamy look on her face. She smiled the entire time and was almost using his body to balance as they danced. Their bodies fit perfectly on the dance floor, just as they did in bed.

Derek enjoyed watching Nicole's body move when she had abandoned all of her inhibitions. He grabbed onto her hips while she swayed them back and forth to the beat. He loved feeling her hands pressing against his chest. He saw men taking notice and pulled her closer when they did. He would have to get used to this with Nicole. She was sexy without trying and that made her so much more appealing to him, as well as every man that could see her.

They returned to the bar when the dance floor got too crowded and she was ready to finish the last two shots. He could see that she needed to let loose. She leaned into him at one point and tried to whisper, "Everything is starting to spin."

That was his sign that they should go back. He signed for the tab and leaned her into his shoulder as they walked to the apartment. He led her straight into the bedroom and curled up in the bed with her. She immediately fell asleep on top of him. He could watch her sleep every night and it would never get old.

CHAPTER NINETEEN

When Nicole woke up, it felt like her head was going to split in half. Everything was too bright. She covered her eyes as best she could and tried to figure out the last thing she could remember. It had to be dancing with Derek. She hoped she didn't look like an idiot. But, God, could the man move. She should have known he could dance with how good he was in bed. She peeked through her fingers to see if she could find him. He was sitting at the breakfast bar reading a paper. She wondered if he could read Spanish or if there were English newspapers here. He must have heard her move the covers because he instantly got up and brought a bottle of water with two white pills.

"Here, love, take these for your head." He helped sit her up like she was a child. She felt slightly embarrassed.

"Holy hangover, Batman," was all she could think to say.

"That's my girl," he laughed.

She wanted to roll back over and die. Her head flooded with every hangover cure she had ever heard of. She was prepared to try them all. Wasn't there something about bananas? Maybe Derek had one of those sugary sports drinks, probably not. Should she take another shot of tequila? That thought alone made her want to throw up. She decided that first a shower and then fresh air would do her some good.

She tried standing and everything went sideways. How could the room still be spinning the following morning? She practically stumbled into the bathroom and turned on the shower. She brushed her teeth while she walked back into the bedroom to let the shower get hot.

Derek was still sitting on the bed watching her. "You needed that last night. The hangover will go away," he said sweetly.

"It doesn't feel like it right now, but thank you. Dinner was wonderful."

"So was dancing with you." He stood up and kissed her cheek in between her brushing. "Now take a shower. You'll feel better. Can you eat when you're hanging?"

"Your famous toast may stay down." She mustered a smile and walked into the shower. The hot water was just what she needed. But she also knew that she could only stay in there for a minute or the steam would start to make her stomach turn. She washed off the sweat from dancing the night before and let the water hit her face for a few minutes, waiting till her stomach told her it was time to get out. Then she shocked her system by walking straight out of the shower and standing there wet and naked for a bit before she dried herself. She threw on a pair of tan linen pants and an orange tank top. Just like the dress, they somehow fit perfectly.

She saw the bed and couldn't resist crawling back into it and closing her eyes. She could have stayed like that all day. But she knew they were going to head back to Puerto Vallarta, so an all-day nap was out of the question. She groaned and forced herself to get up.

She walked out onto the balcony, hoping that the ocean air would help her feel better. She told herself she was never drinking again and almost immediately laughed at the thought. Everyone said that at least once in their life and no one ever meant it. She took a few deep breaths. Her head had started to clear; now to get the nausea to go away. Derek brought her a piece of toast with avocado and a Bloody Mary.

"This is exactly what I need," she said, sitting down at the tiny table, "Are all your views this gorgeous?" she asked him.

"Yes, they all have water views," he told her.

She could tell that he was watching to see how she was feeling. Getting something into her stomach helped her feel better and probably the Bloody Mary did as well. She curled her legs up under her in the chair. Though she enjoyed the moment, Nicole wished she felt better. She really could get used to an ocean view. She thought of the possible hotel in Chicago and wondered what it would be like to live there. Would she have a view of Lake Michigan? What a great way to start her days, sitting on her balcony, drinking a cup of coffee. Her current apartment was in the River North area- a great view of the city but no water view. Now she wanted one.

It would be strange to be there if Derek wasn't. She wondered if he would still stay at other hotels for months at a time. Would she visit him on weekends? Would he come see her for extended periods in Chicago? How would this work? She really couldn't imagine them being apart, but she had to be realistic about this as well. It had been literally a week since they had met. They both admitted to falling in love quickly, but this would still be a long distance relationship and they needed to figure out the logistics of it all.

Once she felt well enough, they went down to meet Hector waiting for them with his car. Nicole was going to miss this hotel. She hoped they'd come back soon. She couldn't wait to wear more of the clothes stored in the closet. She secretly wished she had a bag with her; she would have brought some back to the Paraíso. She wondered if she could hire Maria as a personal shopper on occasion. She should have just asked about the clothes; Derek wouldn't care if she brought some with her. She did pack hastily back in Chicago. She shrugged it off, remembering that they could always go shopping again on the Malecon.

She kept her window down, hoping it would help her complete her recovery. They reached the Paraíso in no time and as she got out of the car, she couldn't help looking over at the Playa Vallarta. She wondered if she'd ever be able to look at it the same way again. She wanted to. It was important to her because of her father and because it was where she met Derek. It was important to Derek not only because of her, but because it was where he had met Roger Long and where the idea of his company had been born.

Derek took her hand, snapping her back into reality. She couldn't wait to get inside, having dreamt about that bed for the entire drive back. Derek opened the door and let her in first. She smiled at the sight of the large modern décor. She really did love this place. She walked straight into the bedroom, climbed into the bed like it was her own, and let out a groan.

"You poor thing. Please try and sleep for a bit." He sat next to her and rubbed her head.

In the quiet, she heard her phone vibrate in her purse. The ringer must have gotten turned off when she threw her phone yesterday. She asked Derek to grab it for her. Nicole glanced at the screen and saw a crazy amount of missed calls and text messages, all from Kate. She shot up in bed, yelling "SHIT!"

"What is it?" Derek sounded concerned.

"I don't know. Kate's been calling and texting. Let me check." She opened up the texts first, to get an idea of what was going on. Her heart began to sink. Andrew had called Kate and told her he was on his way to Vallarta. He had searched the names of the hotels online until one sounded familiar and he recognized Playa Vallarta from her stories. Of course, now he remembered! He was going to be here today, having skipped his meeting and taken the early flight out.

Nicole wasn't sure how to explain it all, so she handed Derek her phone so he could read the numerous texts that filled her screen. He stood as he read and began pacing the room. She wasn't exactly sure what his reaction would be. She knew he was capable of protectiveness on all levels. She had seen his reactions to everything from a shop keeper innocently touching her arm to a man attempting to rape her. She knew his reaction would fall somewhere between those two, she just didn't know how bad it would be. She didn't want to see Andrew or talk to him either. She couldn't believe he decided to come. What the hell was he thinking?

Derek hadn't set the phone down, but he was speechless while he paced. She grabbed the landline by the bed and quickly dialed Kate's number.

"Hey, it's me," she said, "I'm calling from Derek's. I'm sorry, my phone was on silent."

"What are you going to do? Is he there yet?" Kate sounded just as freaked out as Nicole was.

"No, I don't think so. We just got back. I haven't even heard your voice mails. Derek is reading your texts right now. He's pacing. Kate, this isn't good." She watched him as he walked around like he was in a trance, like he didn't even hear her talking about him.

"Why the fuck did he decide to come now?" Kate said. Nicole loved her for being so worried.

"I don't know. I can't deal with this right now. I feel like death from drinking last night. I just want him to go away. Nothing he says can change my mind about this."

"By the way, have you looked up your new man on the Internet yet?" Kate interjected, "I did and good for you, Nic, he's gorgeous. At least he was when he was a UFC fighter."

"He still is," she smiled at Kate's reaction, "When I'm done figuring out this mess, I'll definitely need to do that. I haven't seen those pictures yet. I want to see what he looked like that long ago. I promise to get a picture of us and send it. Don't post it!"

Kate laughed, "Okay. Call me if you need me. Otherwise, let me know what happens. Love you."

And she was gone.

Nicole hung up and watched Derek. She wasn't sure what to say. Her head hurt so badly and this definitely made her feel like she wanted to throw up. She was sick of exes messing with her trip. First, it was Silvia and now Andrew.

"Are you kidding me? What the hell?" she said, not really caring if Derek was listening. She was more talking to the universe anyway. "Why can't I just have a nice vacation and enjoy myself? Is that too much to ask?" She looked up at the sky, waiting for a reply from the gods.

Derek glanced over at her, took his phone out of his pocket, and dialed a number.

"Hector, *cabrón*. I need you to watch for a man coming to the hotel looking for Nicole…Yes, call me immediately…*Gracias*." He ended the call and finally looked over at Nicole, his face transforming from a stony expression to a man in love. He came over and sat next to her on the bed. He leaned her into his chest and began stroking her hair again. He must have been listening to her talk to Kate, because he said calmly, "I know you won't be able to sleep, but please try to relax and feel better? Will you let me handle this?"

"What do you mean by 'handle'?" Visions of him hitting Silvia's cousin popped into her head.

"I want to speak to him, that's all. You don't need to worry. I promise not to go crazy." He kissed her head, needing to know what she was thinking.

"I don't know, Derek. This is my mess, not yours."

She wasn't sure she was comfortable with the idea of the two men discussing her. It all just seemed too weird. Was Derek going to offer Andrew a goat for her hand? Plus, Andrew would freak out. She needed to make sure that Derek wasn't thinking she couldn't handle it. "You know I can deal with Andrew, right?" she asked.

"Of course, love. I would bet you're a force to be reckoned with when crossed." He kissed her nose. "Your messes are my messes now. You said yourself that you can't deal with this today. When Hector calls, let *me* deal with it. I wouldn't push this much if you felt better. Please!"

Why was it that when he said the word *please*, she would give him whatever he asked?

"Oh, whatever. I can't believe I'm saying this but…you can talk to him. Don't be a jerk though, just tell him that I don't want to see him and there is no reason for him to be here."

"I will act like someone worthy of having your love. Don't worry; this isn't a dick-measuring contest. I just don't want you to have to deal with this. You already told him it was over. I will simply tell him, man-to-man, that he had his chance with you and now it is my turn to make you happy."

"Thank you." She leaned over and kissed his cheek. Then she laid back down, grabbed the white comforter, and threw it over her head. "Now just leave me here to die, please."

He let out a laugh and kissed the mound of white that was probably her head and walked out of the room.

CHAPTER TWENTY

Derek was in bed, Nicole resting on his shoulder. She had finally fallen asleep again. He knew she was worried about the situation. He wasn't thrilled about it himself. He didn't want to fight the guy; he wasn't in the fighting cage anymore. He simply wanted to explain to him that Nicole was no longer his concern. But what if he didn't take it well? What was Derek prepared to do? He looked down at her, sleeping calmly, and knew he'd do anything for her. He would do whatever it took to make her happy.

It had been just over an hour and he had his head leaned back with his eyes closed when his text message alert went off. He slipped his phone out of his pocket so that he wouldn't wake up Nicole. It was from Hector. He rolled his eyes and opened the text: "He's here, waiting in the bar."

Derek leaned over and kissed Nicole's head. For her sake, he really would try and be nice. If he came across like a complete asshole, it would make her look stupid. He didn't want anyone thinking poorly of her, even an ex-boyfriend.

He slid his body out from underneath Nicole and she snuggled into the spot where he had been. Even hung over and sleeping, she looked beautiful. He quietly gathered his things and left the apartment without disturbing her. He hoped he would return with Andrew headed back to the airport before she woke.

He stopped on the way out for a shot of tequila. It was only noon, but he needed something to give him an edge. The shot glass was barely back on the bar before he headed for the Playa Vallarta. As he passed Hector, he said hello and swore he could see a smirk come across his face. He hoped that little man wasn't laughing at him. This may not be as serious or dangerous as the Silvia situation, but it still was a pain in his ass.

He knew exactly who Andrew was before he even saw his face. He was the idiot sitting at the bar wearing a pair of khakis and a Hawaiian style shirt, with the type of beer that only Americans drank. In the few seconds before he reached him, Derek tried to figure out what Nicole saw in the man. He was classically handsome, he would give him that. But he looked like he was trying too hard to fit the part. Was Nicole supposed to think that because he was wearing a Hawaiian shirt, he was now this laid back guy that could make her happy? One look at the man and Derek knew Andrew couldn't do that.

Derek noticed that Andrew sat facing directly towards the elevator, barely taking his eyes off the doors. He must have been expecting Nicole to come out of them. Cracking his neck, Derek walked up and sat down on the bar stool next to him, glad it wasn't his favorite one.

"Can I buy you a real beer?" he said to him with a straight face. Not knowing what was going to happen, he put on his fighting face from years back.

"I'm sorry, do I know you?" Andrew looked a bit confused.

"Well, you know of me," Derek answered, "Nicole will not be coming down to speak with you."

"So you're the guy, huh?" Andrew looked like he was ready for a fight. Not that he would win, but he was ready. "Did you tell her she wasn't allowed to see me?"

"Of course I didn't. She's not feeling well from celebrating last night. She's sleeping it off at my place." He couldn't help adding in the last part. This guy was a schmuck.

"You can't make me leave. I'm going to talk to Nicole." Andrew's voice rose and he didn't seem comfortable with it.

"You're going to talk to me. There are some things that I would like to discuss with you," Derek replied calmly. He had the upper hand. Now he could toy with him or get straight to the point. It felt a lot like being in the cage. Some fights were dominated by one person who had all the power for the entire fight. Some highlighted fights, where a great deal of money changed hands, Derek would hold off ending it to give the audience more of a show. This felt very much the same way.

"What could you possibly have to say to me?" Andrew was asking.

"I have a lot of things to say, in fact." Derek took a drink of the beer that the bartender had brought over without having been asked. Andrew had to have noticed that. "First of all, whether it was Nicole or not, you do not let a woman leave on an International trip unless you know exactly where she will be. Please remember that with your future relationships. You always need to make sure that they are safe." Andrew looked like he was going to try and explain himself but Derek kept talking, not allowing him to speak, "Second, in the future, if your girlfriend loses her parent and the only family she had left, you follow her to the ends of the Earth. If you do not, you will have signed the death certificate on your relationship. I am not the cause of your relationship ending. You are."

That was not all that he had to say, but he figured it was time to see if Andrew had anything to say for himself. For the past week, Derek had racked his brain trying to figure out what type of man wouldn't go on vacation with Nicole and for what reasons. He really was truly interested in his response.

"This really is none of your business," Andrew tried to snap at Derek.

"Well, everything involving Nicole is now my business. Would you like to explain your actions? I will make sure that she hears. I can tell you that this issue weighed heavily on her mind initially." How could he stay silent?

"Nicole and I are very different when it comes to traveling. I don't do it often and she was being too hasty with this trip. No one books a trip to Mexico and leaves the same day." Andrew tried to look superior.

Derek couldn't stop himself. "Well, I do. But then again, my plane is at my disposal whenever I'd like to go somewhere." He didn't smile. It was a fact that his plane could be ready within the hour and he took advantage of that often. But he didn't want to act cocky in the way Andrew had just attempted. So he stayed very calm.

"So it's your money, huh?" Andrew laughed to himself.

"You don't really believe that, do you?" Derek asked him. Not really expecting an answer, he continued, "Nicole doesn't know about my plane yet.

She doesn't know the full extent of what I have. But she will want for nothing. Andrew," it might bother him that Derek knew his name, "You had three years to try to make her happy. You had three years to decide what you wanted with Nicole. I knew after three days. I will make her happy."

"I know what I want now. I can make her happy." Andrew finally started to sound passionate rather than arrogant.

"Stop and really think about Nicole. There is so much to that woman. She needs someone that can appreciate all of her. She needs a man that will get on a plane with her whenever she would like to go somewhere. I get the feeling she had to abandon part of herself. Though I haven't asked her, it's just something I've sensed."

"Don't act like you could know her better than me. I've been with her for three years." Andrew shot back.

When Derek heard that fact, it made it hard for him to keep his composure. He hated thinking of her ever with someone else, even for a night, especially with this guy. Andrew wouldn't even look at him; he just stared ahead. Derek couldn't blame him. Even though this guy was stupid enough to lose Nicole, it had to be hard to know that Derek was with her now. Derek wanted to tell him that he could make her moan his name over and over. But he had told Nicole he wouldn't be petty.

"Listen, I know this is hard for you," he said, "I would die now before I would lose her. But your relationship is over with her. What has happened cannot be taken back. She needs someone like me and I promise you that she will be happy and I will not hurt her."

"I don't need your promises," Andrew said, still not looking at Derek.

"No, you don't. And that's one of the problems. Because I would need one. If Nicole ever decides that she does not want to be with me, I will make sure that the next man treats her well. I can't believe you don't want that for her."

"Don't try to act like the nice guy," Andrew spouted at him, "You took advantage of her in her time of grieving."

That comment also made it very hard to stay calm. "Andrew, I have been nothing but nice to you. But that time has come to an end." He put his hands under the bar because he knew he was balling them into fists. "You left your girlfriend to grieve alone on a trip to remember her only family she had left. Do not blame anyone but yourself for that. I have helped her visit her father's favorite spots and allowed her to talk about him and tell me stories. All things you should have been doing." He took a deep breath. "I told Nicole that I would not act like a jerk. She wants you to know that she doesn't want to see you and there is no reason for you to be here."

"I want to hear her say that to me." Andrew finally looked at him. Now things could get interesting.

Derek stood for effect. He was about the same height as Andrew, but in far better shape. "That's not going to happen. She doesn't want to see you." He raised his voice just enough to sound intimidating, yet not irrational. "She has already been through enough. I will protect her from anyone that would like to add difficulties to her life."

"Well, you can't make me leave. I will get a room here and she'll talk to me at some point. I came all the way here, I'm not leaving." Andrew sounded like a child.

"I cannot make you leave Puerto Vallarta. But I can tell you that you won't be staying here."

"Fine, there's a hotel right across the street." He pointed at the Paraíso.

"Or there," Derek said, beginning to sound aggressive.

"You can't own all of the fucking hotels here. I'll find one and I will sit here and wait for her."

"Why are you doing this to her, Andrew? She doesn't want to see you. I don't think I could be clearer about that fact."

"Because once she sees me, she'll remember our life together." He looked at him like he had something with Nicole that Derek didn't. All in good time, Derek reminded himself.

"She's over her life with you. Seeing you won't change that. In fact, I will have her things taken from your apartment. If rent money is an issue, I will send you a check for her half of the remainder of the lease." He knew he was an attorney and could most likely afford the rent himself. Still, Derek couldn't help emasculating him a little bit.

"Money isn't the issue!" Andrew yelled.

"Well, that's nice to hear." He leaned in a little closer. He had perfected the intimidating move in his fighting days. "If you feel the need to sit and watch us enjoy her vacation from afar, that is your choice. If you'd like to make her uncomfortable on a trip that's about her father, that is your choice. Maybe you'll see that she doesn't need you." He threw enough cash on the table to cover his beer and a tip. "We're done here."

He walked away, toward the Paraíso. He didn't care if Andrew saw him go into the hotel. He could handle him if needed.

CHAPTER TWENTY-ONE

Nicole couldn't believe that Andrew was across the street. What the hell was he thinking? She was honestly surprised that she had no urge to see him at all. Usually she wouldn't let someone else deal with something like this. Then again, she did feel like she'd throw up if she moved. Looking over at the glass wall, she wondered if she had the strength to get up and figure out how to make it disappear like Derek had. The panels must follow some kind of track. But that seemed like too much work, so instead, she threw the covers back over her head and closed her eyes. She wanted everything to go away.

With a sense of relief, she heard the door open. Derek was back and that hadn't taken long at all. Wanting to find out what happened, she called from under the covers as loudly as her body would allow, "You're back. Come get in bed and tell me everything."

"No thanks, I have other plans for us," she heard a woman say, "Get up, Blondie." Her heart stopped for a split second. She couldn't breathe. It was Silvia. It had to be. Nicole slowly lifted the covers back.

Silvia was standing over the bed with a gun pointed straight at her. Nicole tried to tell herself to stay calm, but it wasn't working. What was she supposed to do? She had to think fast. All she could come up with was:

1.Keep her talking.

2.Make Silvia see her as person, not an object.

3.Try to find something in reach that could be used as a weapon.

Nicole slowly backed herself up until she sat against the headboard. Her heart was racing; she felt like she might start hyperventilating.

"You're Silvia," she stated more than asked. Nicole could tell that she had tried to disguise herself. Her hair was cut into a short bob, bleached completely blonde. Why the hell was Silvia calling her Blondie given how she, herself, looked? She was wearing an outfit that made her look like a tourist, which was smart. If she was going to hide in plain sight, it was better to look like someone on vacation. Despite that, Nicole recognized her as the woman who had given her the stink eye when she came in from running a few days before.

"Yes, I'm Silvia," she said, looking around, "This place is pretty nice. He would never bring me here. He would never bring anyone here. What makes you so special?"

Trying to think of something to say, Nicole didn't answer her.

"No, really, what makes you so special?" Silvia started to sound aggravated. She moved the gun around like she was a bit unsteady with it.

"Silvia, he and I are supposed to be together. We knew right away. I even broke up with my boyfriend. You don't need to do this," Nicole told her, trying to keep her calm. She figured from all the movies she had seen that she wasn't going to talk the gun out of her hand. She just needed to stall long enough for Derek to get home. Oh God, what if Silvia shot him when he came in?

She had to be smart about this. She needed to give him a warning somehow.

"Awwww," Silvia mocked, "Well, isn't that sweet," she continued on in Spanish, but Nicole didn't understand. She wasn't very good at this; she was doing the opposite of keeping Silvia calm.

Maybe if she kept Silvia answering questions, it would keep her from using the gun. "How did you know I'd be alone?"

"That was the beautiful part," Silvia responded, "I've been waiting all night for you both. I followed you when you got back this morning. I needed to see which room was his. I didn't think he'd even leave your side. I was waiting for you both to leave so that I could be inside when you got back. And, by luck, I saw him walking across the street this morning without you. I figured this may be my only chance to get you alone."

"What are you going to do?" Nicole pressed on.

"I haven't thought that far ahead," Silvia admitted, "Maybe I'll make you watch us have sex on this bed." She sounded like she was pondering ideas. "I'd bet he'd do just about anything to keep you alive. Even ravish me in front of you. What do you think? Would he do that?"

Oh hell, this woman was crazy. What was the answer she wanted to hear? Nicole really didn't want to play the victim. She wished she knew what time it was. How long had she slept? When would Derek be back?

"I'm sure he would do anything for me," she said, trying to sound strong.

"Hmmmm, I bet he would," Silvia kept the gun on Nicole, but looked around a bit, "I could get used to staying in a place like this. I bet he looks gorgeous walking around here naked. I know he does that. He used to do it when he got us suites at the Playa

Vallarta." She smiled at Nicole, trying to make her jealous.

Nicole wasn't going to let that happen. She needed to keep a cool head. The bed was too big to reach anything to use as a weapon. She had to mark that off the list. She was doing a decent job at getting Silvia to talk. So that left trying to make Silvia see her as a human being with a life to value, and not a thing she could just shoot with a gun.

Not really sure what else to say, she tried, "My father just died. That's why I'm here."

"Oh, I thought you were here to pick up rich men," Silvia snapped.

"Silvia, I didn't even know about all of this. I thought Derek was on vacation from Detroit."

Silvia laughed, "Oh, so he told you his usual lie?"

"He didn't lie. He just told me he was from Detroit. But after I met your cousin, he brought me here." She wanted to yell at the woman but knew that she shouldn't. "I think that jump started things."

"Oh yes, did you like my cousin? He'll be in jail for a bit with that extra present he was trying to give you. A pity, he's a nice guy. Oh well."

All Nicole wanted to say in response was that she was crazy. But she knew that was a bad idea.

"You don't think this stunt will end up with you in jail as well?" she asked honestly.

"Like I said, I'm not thinking that far ahead." Silvia gave her a creepy smile. "Now, what shall we do with you? What would make a statement when Derek arrives? Should I get a knife from the kitchen? We could do something with that pretty face."

Nicole was terrified now. Still, she wasn't tied up and Silvia was pretty small. She knew she wasn't going to be able to hold a gun to her and cut her. What was her plan? If she put down the gun, Nicole could probably fight her off with just a knife. That could work. She needed to stay sharp. She should have gotten some fighting lessons from Derek. What if Silvia had?

"Let's not do anything," she suggested, "Let's wait for Derek to get back so we can all talk." She hoped hearing Derek's name would make that sound like a good idea.

"No, I don't like that plan. Maybe you should take your clothes off. Everyone feels a bit more vulnerable when they're naked." Silvia pointed the gun more directly at her. "Plus, I've just gotta see what Derek is all excited about with you. Too bad I can't invite my cousin over again."

Nicole felt like she was going to faint. This couldn't really be happening. Silvia was absolutely right; she would feel more vulnerable if she was naked. Could she use her clothes as a weapon? If she could get her pants around her neck, she could choke her with them. The gun was the problem; Silvia could shoot her before she had the chance to do anything.

"Strip, bitch!" Silvia yelled.

Nicole slowly lifted her tank top over her head, leaving it just in reach so she could use it later. Then she slowly took off her pants and did the same with them. There she sat, in the beautiful lingerie that Maria had picked up for her in Nuevo Vallarta. At least she had a bra on. She hoped to God that this would satisfy Silvia. What little coverage she had, she wanted to keep.

"Well, well. Aren't you pretty?" Silvia said, "You know I've always had a thing for beautiful women. It's one of the perks of my job. I get to see their tight bodies in little bikinis all over the place. I heard about your dress the other night. I would have loved to see those tits in that dress."

Nicole's face went numb. She tried to remember that Silvia was much smaller than her cousin. She wouldn't have been able to fight him off, but she could stop Silvia.

"Forget the knife, let's find some way to tie up those hands and legs. Maybe I could have some fun with you." Keeping the gun trained on Nicole, she quickly looked around the room. "Derek is far too casual to have any ties in that closet. That's a shame. I want to spread those legs wide."

"You're not going to touch me!" Nicole yelled. She was more angry than scared now. She wasn't going to let this happen. She was going to go down fighting at least. She grabbed the edge of her pants without Silvia noticing and started to stand up on her knees. She didn't really think that Silvia would shoot her. Some people are murders, but most aren't. Very few people cross that line. She was banking on the fact that Silvia wasn't one.

"I'm the one with the gun. I'll be deciding what happens here today and what doesn't," Silvia said in a superior voice.

Just as she did, they both heard the door unlocking. Before she could think, Nicole said as calmly as possible, "Hi, honey. How was your talk with John? I'm sick to death of dealing with exes." She hoped that Derek would catch on to her clues. Immediately Silvia raced toward her and put the gun to her head.

CHAPTER TWENTY-TWO

Derek froze in his tracks. This could not be happening. Nicole was a smart girl. He wondered who was in there with her. It couldn't be Silvia's cousin; he was in custody. Gael still hadn't been able to track down Silvia herself and Nicole may have referenced exes for a reason. Instinct kicked in; he needed to get help up here.

"Hi, love," he called back, "I'll be right in. I'm just grabbing a drink from the fridge. John is fine."

He needed to give himself a second. He opened the refrigerator door and hummed naturally to himself. Then he opened his phone contacts and sent a text message to Gabriel, the manager of the Paraíso: "Bring gun in safe to my room quickly. Say you're room service. Call police. Someone has Nicole." He grabbed a bottle of water and closed the door, trying to figure out his next move. He couldn't leave her in there alone any longer.

He walked in to see one of his worst nightmares. Silvia had Nicole, down to her bra and panties, a gun to her head. Nicole looked terrified, but was trying to hide it. It was amazing how quickly he knew things like that about her. Her eyes weren't red; she hadn't cried yet. She was staying strong. He cracked his neck to each side, trying to keep it together.

"Honey, we have a guest." She tried to diffuse the tension and he loved her for it.

"I see that. Are you okay?" he asked, wanting to make sure that Silvia hadn't hurt her. He didn't like that she was undressed.

"Oh blah, blah, blah, she's fine!" Silvia said, rolling her eyes, "But she may not be for long."

"You're mad at me, Silvia, not Nicole. Keep her out of this." Where the hell was Gabriel? Derek tried to stay as close to the bedroom door as he could so that he'd be able to get to the incoming gun.

"I could have gotten you back if she hadn't shown up. You were noticing me again," Silvia responded with a mixture of anger and sadness.

"No, I wasn't. We didn't have anything in common but the Playa Vallarta. You are a nice girl, just not the right one for me." He tried to sound sincere. Silvia was bat shit crazy, but right now, he was focusing on keeping her from hurting Nicole.

He was making eye contact with Nicole as much as he could without upsetting Silvia. He had to balance the two as long as he could. "Now let her go," he said, "You can put the gun to my head if it will make you feel better."

"No, she won't!" Nicole yelled.

"Isn't she just the sweetest?" Silvia mocked. "She's trying to protect her man. Before you arrived, we were trying to figure out what to do for fun." His entire body tensed at the thought of how sadistic that conversation probably was. How scared was Nicole on the inside? She was still doing a great job of hiding it.

Just as Silvia was about to speak again, there was a knock at the door and a woman called in a sweet voice, "Room service!" Thank God, Derek thought.

"I had some champagne sent up," he explained, "I'll get rid of her." He hoped that Silvia bought it. He didn't even look at Nicole in case Silvia got suspicious that he was trying to send her a nonverbal message.

"Go, get rid of her now," she yelled, pointing the gun quickly from Nicole to him and back to Nicole, "She'll stay right here with me."

"I'll be right back," he said to Nicole and ran to the door. He opened it; there was Gabriel holding the gun. The brave housekeeper had a pleasant voice, but he could see in her eyes that she was terrified. Derek began his dialogue for Silvia, "We've changed our minds. Would you please take this back?"

As he spoke, Gabriel mouthed to him that the police were on their way. Derek took the gun and walked back inside, tucking it behind his back in the waistband of his pants. Though Derek had only ever done target shooting, he was a decent shot. But outside of the gun range, he dealt with problems with his fists. This would be his first time using a weapon outside of a controlled environment. Still, he was prepared to do what was needed.

He cracked his neck to each side again and walked back into the bedroom before Silvia could get suspicious. He thought if he could distract her enough he could pull the gun and shoot her before she'd have a chance to hurt Nicole. He wasn't ready to kill her; he figured her shoulder was a good spot. He saw her fondling Nicole's breast with the gun and Nicole smacking it away. The whole thing just made him sick to his stomach, but he was so impressed with how Nicole was handling it all.

"Okay, I'm back. *Don't touch her*!" he growled, "Let her go."

"No, I think I want her to do a strip tease for me. Wouldn't you like to see that too?" Silvia sneered again.

"She's not doing anything. Silvia, you're not going to shoot anyone. You know how many hotel guests would hear the shot? There's no way you'd get away," he said. What the hell was she thinking? He needed to figure out how to distract her and get the gun faced away from Nicole, "If you want either of us to do anything, you're going to have to put the gun down."

Silvia didn't answer. She looked like she was trying to decide what to do next. At least she didn't refuse immediately. That had to be a good thing.

"Come on, Silvia, put it down. We'll figure this out together," he said in a quiet tone. Maybe referring to them together would have an effect. Silvia slowly started to waiver, lowering the gun a little. She was thinking about her options. "That's my girl," he said, remembering that he had called her that sometimes when they dated because she was so tiny.

She smiled at him and he knew she remembered as well. He watched her movements closely. As recognition hit her face, she must have forgotten about holding the gun because her arm dropped from the weight of it so that the barrel pointed to the floor.

Before she had time to react, Derek pulled the gun and shot Silvia in the shoulder. She screamed from the shock of the pain and the gun fell out of her hand. Her other hand came up to cover the wound. Nicole jumped off the bed. Derek kicked the gun toward her, keeping his weapon pointed at Silvia.

He had done it. Nicole was safe and Silvia was disarmed. Silvia was screaming at him in Spanish, but Derek stayed cold-faced, aiming right at her head. He freed Nicole without killing Silvia, but if she tried to hurt Nicole again, he wouldn't hesitate.

"How are you holding up, love?" he asked Nicole without looking at her. "The police will be here soon. Just hang in there. You can get dressed now."

Nicole walked up behind him to stay out of his aim, whispering that she loved him. She kissed his shoulder and set the gun on the dresser behind them. She quickly dressed and stood beside him. They waited like that, stuck in time, until the police arrived.

When the police did show up, it was a chaotic scene. They kicked the door in, guns drawn, screaming *"Policía!"* Everything started happening at once and with lots of screaming. Two officers went over and secured Silvia. She was surrounded by blood at this point, a huge contrast from the white room. There was no official reading of rights or anything like that in Mexico. They just pushed her over and slapped cuffs on her wrists. They were not gentle with her wound and Derek couldn't have cared less. A female officer went to Nicole.

Derek realized he was still facing the gun at Silvia when a man yelled at him to drop it. He looked up and saw a gun pointed at him in precaution. He raised his free arm in surrender and slowly bent down to put his weapon on the floor. When he did, he put the other hand up and backed away. As soon as he was out of reach of it, the officer lowered his gun and took the one from the floor. Derek apologized to the officer. The man didn't seem to hold a grudge.

He walked over to check on Nicole. The woman was taking her story. He sat down next to her, but tried not to interrupt anything. He looked up and saw Gael walk in. Telling Nicole that he'd be right back, he ran over, asking, "Did Gabriel call you?"

"Yes. Sorry I couldn't get her in time, *amigo*. She went off the grid." He seemed worried Derek was going to yell at him. "She looks like shit as a blonde," he added.

"Just make sure wherever they take her, she doesn't come back," Derek told him and put a hand on his arm to show there were no hard feelings. This wasn't Gael's fault. Together, they watched Silvia get taken away in hand cuffs. Both officers acknowledged Gael as they passed him.

"I still have connections with the agency. I'll make sure I get to interrogate her and have a say in what happens," Gael told him.

"We're in Mexico, *amigo*. I don't really want to know what happens to her. Just make sure she doesn't come back," Derek informed him.

"I will make certain she doesn't."

Derek looked back toward Nicole. Watching her talk about the incident, she seemed very disconnected from everything. He hoped she wasn't going to disconnect herself from him as well. This was a lot for anyone to take. Attacked by a crazy man, then held and practically molested at gunpoint by a crazy bitch. He hoped she wasn't ready to leave Puerto Vallarta and him behind and run as fast as she could back to Chicago. He couldn't blame her for wanting to go back to a normal life. Andrew was most likely still across the street. Would he blame her if she went running back into his arms?

It looked like the officer was finished asking her questions. Nicole saw him coming over to her and gave him a sweet smile. He sat down next to her on the bed.

"I'm so sorry this happened. She's in custody and Gael assured me she isn't coming back."

She leaned her head on his shoulder. "That's good."

They sat there quietly while the officers finished their work. Gael handled everything with them so that Derek could focus Nicole and he was grateful for that. Gael even made sure all of the blood was cleaned. Derek wanted everyone to leave. There had never been this many people in his apartment and he didn't like it. His apartments were his fortress of solitude and he was only ready to share them with Nicole. He wanted to curl up with her in the bed with all of the windows opened. They could listen to the ocean and the sounds of people on the beach. He wanted Nicole to be okay. He couldn't tell what was going through her mind and he hoped that she would tell him.

Finally, it was quiet, just the two of them still sitting on the bed.

"Do you want to talk about it?" he asked her.

She looked apprehensive at first. But next thing he knew, she was crying and telling him everything that had happened. He figured that she must have been holding everything in and now she could fall apart. It was very hard to listen to, but he knew that it was no comparison to Nicole living through it. He wanted to kick himself. He thought he was protecting her by talking to Andrew and she was left to deal with Silvia on her own.

He had no idea that Silvia was into women, either. She joked a few times about having a threesome, but always made it sound like it would be to please him. He wasn't into that kind of thing. He usually would never wish bad things on people, but he couldn't help think that she'd be getting all kinds of female attention if she ended up in a Mexican prison. He honestly didn't care. She needed to pay for what she did and had threatened to do.

When Nicole caught him up on what happened before he got there, she took a deep breath. She had needed to get it out, but now all the tears seemed to be gone. She asked, "How did you manage to save the day this time? Where did you get the gun? And the police?"

"When you called Andrew 'John' and mentioned exes, I knew you were trying to warn me. I sent a text to the manager, Gabriel, for help while I was getting water out of the fridge."

"Thank God you caught on. This could have ended badly. I hated hearing you call her 'your girl', but I know why you did it."

"It was hard to say, but it seemed like the only thing that would work. You're my only love now." He kissed her head. "Does it feel like a stay-in-bed-all-day kind of day?" he asked her, "I can open up all of the windows to the patio."

"Yes, I would love that. I'd like to take a shower first," she replied. He kissed her and she stood up. "Would you tell me what happened with Andrew when I get back?"

"I'll tell you everything."

He wasn't sure how she would take Andrew saying he wouldn't leave. She didn't need any more drama. That he knew for sure.

CHAPTER TWENTY-THREE

Nicole stayed in the shower for a long time, the events of the day tumbling through her head. She tried to stay positive. Derek had talked to Andrew and Silvia was in custody. There shouldn't be any more road blocks for them, other than the fact that she lived in Chicago and he lived in hotels around the world. After everything that happened with Silvia, that problem seemed easy enough to figure out.

When she got out of the shower, she wrapped herself in the big white robe that Derek had set out for her. She went back into the bedroom, where all of the windows were open. Derek had made them a pot of coffee and had set extra pillows out on the oversized chaise, the spot where they made love for the first time in this apartment. He walked up to her with a steaming cup of coffee, "I thought I'd have all of this bedding replaced today. For now, would you like to sit out on the balcony for a while?"

"That sounds wonderful," she replied, "Come tell me what happened with Andrew."

They snuggled up on the chaise. Nicole was worried that she might spill coffee on the stark white cushion. But Derek said, "It can be replaced. Enjoy yourself." So she settled in. He continued, "Andrew wasn't very receptive to the idea of discussing anything with me."

"That doesn't surprise me." She burrowed herself into Derek's shoulder as far as she could.

"He thinks that I used your situation to my advantage. He's here to get you back and he knows that he wants you. I explained that I didn't take advantage of you during your grieving. I also explained to him that he should have found out where you would be traveling for safety's sake and that he should have come with you. I told him that I was there with you while you remembered your father."

"How did he take that?" she said, in between sips of coffee.

"He wasn't happy, but I did finally get him to explain why he didn't come."

"Really?" she was interested to hear what Andrew had to say for himself.

"He said that he didn't travel often and he thought you were too hasty in your plans. That was it."

"Seems like a perfectly good reason to lose a girlfriend," she tried to joke.

"There's another thing." Derek hesitated and she wasn't sure why. "He said he's not leaving. He's waiting to see you in person."

Nicole just closed her eyes, wondering what to do. Part of her wanted to walk down there right now in her fluffy bathrobe and slippers and explain that she was perfectly fine without him. Part of her wanted to let him wait here until he died. "Hmmmm," was the only audible sound she could muster.

"Want to think about it later?"

"Yes, I do. I want to enjoy the quiet with you for now."

He set both of their coffee cups down. The sun was higher over them in the sky and Nicole started to feel hot in the robe. "No one can see us, right?" she asked.

"Not a soul, love."

She took off her robe and laid back to let the sun hit her whole body. "I could get used to this!" She peeked up at him and he laughed. With the sun overhead, she could only see his silhouette.

"I took a look at your list again," he said, "What do you think about hiding away inside today and spending the whole day tomorrow checking things off of it? We've had a few distractions, but now we can get back to it."

She still couldn't see his face from the brightness of the sun, so she sat up to be at eye level with him again, "Yes, even with all of the shit that has happened, I still want to explore Vallarta for my dad."

"Then we will." He leaned over and kissed her deeply. Although she was naked, his hands did very little exploring. He grabbed onto the side of her hip, but it stayed there firmly. She knew he wasn't going to make love to her after what had just happened and appreciated him for it. Even though the man would always excite her, she also knew that this wasn't the time. She loved that their connection was more than physical.

When he slowed and ended the kiss, he looked at her. "Any way I could get you to stay a little longer? One more week is not long enough."

She nestled back into him again and soaked up the moment. "I have to get back to work," she said.

"Do you miss it?" he asked her.

"Yes I do," she replied, realizing that it wasn't the job she missed, but rather the writing itself. She had caught herself over the last few days thinking of how she'd describe things and how she'd set a scene. All of her writing over the past few years had been about other people's weddings. She enjoyed it, but she did miss getting to use her imagination the way she did in college. There was a time when she saw herself as an author more than a columnist. Nicole hadn't thought about that in a long time. She wanted to clarify her answer, so she added, "Well, I miss writing more than the job."

"You know, you could write anywhere." He kissed the top of her head. "If there was a place that inspired you, I would take you there."

"Yes, that's a good point."

"Will you at least think about it?" he asked sweetly.

"Yes, of course," she said and closed her eyes again to enjoy lying naked in the sun.

She wondered about Derek's offer. If she left her job, she would have no means of income at the moment. That scared her a little bit. She didn't really have unpaid bills right now. She wasn't in credit card debt and she didn't have a car. Her bills mainly consisted of half of what it cost to live in the apartment with Andrew, a phone bill, a gym membership, and her city bus pass. She wasn't going to be living with Andrew anymore, but where would she live instead? She had to consider that. Even if a dream of writing novels just crept into her head, how would she support herself until then?

She remembered a conversation that she had with her father when she was choosing colleges. She hadn't thought of it in years. When she told her dad that she wanted to write, he asked if she would dedicate her first book to him. She hadn't even really expected to be an author. She wasn't exactly sure what she was going to do with a degree once she had it, but she always thought she'd have to find a job writing to support herself. That was how she ended up working at *Chicago Home Magazine*.

Then she remembered watching the wedding setup in Nuevo Vallarta. What a fun wedding to write about. But who would she write it for? As far as she knew, there wasn't any type of paper or magazine that wrote about destination weddings. Even on the Internet, the information was usually about the location and not a particular wedding itself. She would have to look into some options and see if it already existed or if there was even a market for something like that.

Derek made them a pitcher of mojitos and brought Nicole out some sun screen and her bathing suit cover-up. They sat in the sun and talked for most of the afternoon. This time it wasn't about their pasts or stories that you tell people when you're getting to know them. This time it felt like they had known each other forever. They laughed together. It was hard to believe how they had started their day. It was one hundred percent different than the moment they were having together.

This was the first time in her life, other than with her father, that she thought she had a real partnership with someone. Someone she could get through anything with. She had a gun pointed at her head a mere few hours ago. Derek had saved her again and made sure that her life returned to normal as fast as she wanted it to. She was able to cry about it and he truly listened. He let her set the pace of the day. He let her decide when she didn't need to dwell on the moment anymore. Had Silvia somehow gotten away, Nicole would probably still be a mess. But Silvia was gone for good now and

Nicole didn't care where she was taken, as long as they threw away the key.

Nicole did want to follow up with Derek about that another time. She wanted to make sure that they would be informed if Silvia was allowed out of prison. The nice thing was that Silvia didn't seem to know about Derek's other properties. If Silvia did get out, Nicole wouldn't return to Vallarta with him. She'd visit him at another property. Though she hoped it wouldn't come to that.

When it was late afternoon, Nicole decided she wanted to find out if Andrew really had waited for her next door. "Can we take a shower and go see if Andrew is still over there waiting?" She glanced significantly in the direction of the Playa Vallarta and smiled. "I'd like to get the issues with both of our exes settled today."

"Would you like to go alone?" he inquired. He didn't seem tense about that option, but she hadn't thought about that yet.

"I'm not sure. Do you want to come?"

"I'd prefer it, but it's your call. I've seen how well you can handle yourself."

She laughed, taking his hand and leading him into the bathroom. She turned on the shower to let the water heat up and lifted his t-shirt over his head. Then she unsnapped his board shorts. They were already rather loose and with a tiny tug, they fell to the floor. Derek lifted her sheer cover-up over her head. He grabbed her by the back of the neck and pulled her in for a long kiss. He whispered in her ear how much he loved her. Without stopping the kiss, they moved together into the shower. The water fell over their heads as he kissed her neck. Derek moved them toward the tile wall of the shower. He lifted her up and she wrapped her legs around him. She held onto him for dear life while they made love passionately, water rushing all around them. While the steam billowed, Derek made her climax over and over until her body clung to him, limp from exhaustion. It was the perfect motivation to tell Andrew to go home.

CHAPTER TWENTY-FOUR

Derek watched Nicole with amazement while Hector made his way to the Malecon. They were having dinner at the current trendy spot that night, one with a rooftop area with gorgeous views of the city and ocean. Nicole had handled Andrew with such class. Derek thought it would be awkward to be there while they talked, but she had made it easy. And, with everything that she said to him, he didn't think that Andrew could deny it was over. No matter how much he wanted to win her back, he couldn't prevent her happiness. Ultimately it came down to the fact that Andrew wasn't the right one for her. And she felt that way regardless of Derek. Nicole had given Andrew a hug, kissed his cheek platonically, and wished him well. He knew it was over and left for the airport.

Derek had sat out on the balcony for a while, while Nicole called Kate. She sat in the living room, where he couldn't help but hear the conversation. She explained everything to Kate, from Derek's talk with Andrew to Silvia holding them at gunpoint and Nicole ending it with Andrew in person. Derek chuckled to himself when she made him sound like a hero, alerting Gabriel and getting a hold of a gun. Sometimes she was too cute for words. Although he couldn't hear Kate's responses, it sounded like the friend was quite relieved that it was all over.

Kate had updated Nicole on their friends' lives over the past week and a half. There was an on again, off again couple that was currently on again. He thought their names were Jenny and Matt, but wasn't positive.

He liked hearing Nicole connect with her friends again. He wanted Nicole to live with him, but never expected her to abandon all of her friends. He had the means to send Nicole back to Chicago as much as possible or to bring her friends to her. If the Chicago hotel deal went through, it would be an added bonus, since he and Nicole could stay in Chicago for part of the year. Derek had to admit to himself that he hoped she'd want to be somewhere warm for the winter, but he was willing to do anything to make her happy. They could stock their Chicago apartment with loads of winter clothes.

He was getting ahead of himself again. It was so easy for him to include her in his plans for the future. Oh, this woman!

When the call with Kate was done, they visited a few of her father's favorite places. Due to everything the day before, they didn't plan anything beyond casual shopping and enjoying some fun times at his watering holes. The two of them were doing a fair amount of day drinking, trying to pack in all of Old Bill's favorites into one visit. He had a feeling that Nicole's father didn't drink as much as they two were, trying to catch up. It was worth it, though.

Now Hector was pulling the car up to the restaurant. Derek realized that he had been deep in thought for the entire drive, though it hadn't been far. He relished the fact that he and Nicole could be together and not need to fill the air with idle conversation. She was probably thinking about things as well. Hector held the door for them both and Derek took her hand as they walked into the restaurant.

The décor of the place always reminded him a bit of his Vallarta apartment: minimalistic and white everywhere. They even had white sheets of material along the walls to add some softness. He and Nicole were taken up the stairs just past the hostess stand. He watched Nicole's face as they stepped out onto the rooftop dining space. It was one of the best views of the Malecon. You could see much further from up above. The same white decoration scheme continued up there. There were some VIP sections with large white u-shaped couches with white sheets separating each area. There were ropes blocking off each one. If Nicole wanted to stay and have a drink, he would pay whatever was needed to get past those ropes. Usually it required bottle service: a couple hundred dollars for a bottle of alcohol with all the mixers you'd like and the area was yours for the night.

There was a bar, tiled all in white, with white bar stools and cocktail tables scattered close by. The dining tables were closer to the edge of the balcony for the best view, in addition to a few white chaise lounges very similar to his where guests could relax and converse while they enjoyed drinks.

Their table was at the corner of the balcony, where they could see the furthest. Nicole looked perfect. Her brightly colored blue dress, strapless and reaching to her knees, made her stand out even more than her beauty itself. Her hair was down and the long blond strands swayed in the breeze. As Derek sat across from her, he watched her look over the Malecon in wonder. "Are you still happy here?" he asked. After everything that had happened, he was honestly wondering.

She looked at him and thought for a moment about her answer. "Yes, I am. This was my dad's favorite place. I'm not going to let Silvia ruin that."

Derek really did admire how strong she was. "I'm glad," he told her, "I love it here but would not return if it was too hard for you. Are you still excited to mark off more things on your list tomorrow?"

"Yes, I need another day all about Dad." Derek had noticed that she had been referring to him as "Dad" more than "my father" now. He wondered if she used the more casual term because they were more comfortable with each other.

Derek wanted her to stay with him permanently. He tried to find a way to bring it up. "I've been thinking about your father and what Kate said the first time you told her about me," he said, "I had the pleasure of meeting Andrew. I'm sure he is a very good man, but you seem like you do need more in your life. It sounds like you have your father's wandering spirit and would love to travel the world and see different things."

Nicole smiled at him. "For most people there isn't an option of living all over the world. It never occurred to me to let one place get old. But I can see where living in different places could be fun. Keep things fresh. I thought it might be interesting to look into options to write about specific destination weddings."

Her mind was already on the same track as his. "There is something I've been considering since we saw the wedding setup at the Samba. What would you think about writing for weddings on my properties?" Nicole didn't answer, but he saw her eyes lit up, so he continued, "I've been thinking that we could add a section to the literature about the hotels, in print and online. I would have to see which of the owners would be receptive to the idea. It would help narrow down where we could visit next." He added the last part in there to see if she was open to the idea of doing this for the foreseeable future.

"I wonder if they would. That's exactly the kind of idea I was considering. All the information on destination weddings seems to focus purely on the location and venue itself. I don't think anyone has focused on the couple and the specific weddings themselves yet. You'd really do that for me?" She had puppy dog eyes by the time she finished.

"Of course I would. Love, I've been trying to find a way to get you to stay with me." He took both of her hands in his and asked, "Will you consider it?"

She took a moment to think and, though he would have loved her to scream yes, he was glad that she was truly considering whether it was the right thing to do. She looked out at the water, pondering the idea. Then she looked into his eyes and gave him a beautiful smile and he knew her answer before she said it.

"I'd like that," she said simply.

Derek had never felt happiness like this before. All in that one moment, everything seemed brighter. Everything went out of focus around her; Nicole was the only thing he could see. He still had her hands, so he gestured for her to come to him. She stood up and he pulled her around the table into his lap. She giggled, but didn't look around to see if anyone was watching. They were all that mattered.

She sat on his lap and rested her arms on each shoulder. He swept a strand of hair out from her face and took her mouth into his. It felt like it was their first kiss again, at that little bar on the beach. He knew he could kiss her forever. When the kiss slowed down, she kept her body close. She leaned her forehead into his and had her eyes closed. It was amazing how far they had come in one day. Keeping her body against his, she spoke, "Do you know what else I'd love to do?"

"Tell me."

"I'd love to write a book. I'm glad you're offering to help keep me employed. That's important to me. But I feel like I have a book inside of me. This way, you will give me the opportunity to find it."

"I'm sure there may be many books inside that beautiful head of yours. I look forward to reading them." He kissed her again. He noticed that the waiter appeared to be giving them privacy. He knew that Nicole was hungry, so he suggested they take a look at the menu.

They drank white wine and Nicole joked that it was a good choice because it matched the décor. The restaurant offered a tapas menu and the two of them must have tried every dish on it. The meal took all night. They began with goat cheese in a tomato sauce with *crostini* to dip. They shared bacon-wrapped dates and paella with prawns poached in a white wine sauce. They sampled an array of different meats, seared and served with all types of reduction sauces. They shared potatoes prepared in mouthwatering sauces.

They talked about where to visit next and what type of book she'd like to write. Derek couldn't believe that this was happening. He had been trying to prepare himself for a long distance relationship. He would have made it work, but he wasn't sure how hard it would be. Now he didn't have to. Now he'd have her with him every day.

After endless dishes and two bottles of wine, they decided to go back to their apartment. They were both drunk, though not nearly as bad as their tequila night at the Samba. Hector was waiting by the car in front of the restaurant when they walked outside.

"Can we walk for a bit?" she asked him sweetly.

"You heard the boss, Hector. We'll be back in a little bit." Hector smiled and got back into the front seat of the car. Derek held Nicole's hand while they crossed the busy street to walk along the water. He put his arm around her and she leaned into his shoulder.

They wandered in silence, taking in the surroundings. The night was gorgeous. He could not wait to do this with her in endless towns around the world. She hadn't even agreed to be his wife and he could already imagine them honeymooning in Venice. She would love it there.

When they made their way back to the restaurant, Hector was there waiting and drove them to the hotel. Nicole had apologized profusely for making him wait, though Hector could not have been nicer about it. Derek was going to miss him while they were gone. Early on in their business relationship, Derek had officially put him on his payroll so that he would get paid even when Derek was not in Vallarta. He didn't like thinking of him struggling to take care of his wife and two little sons. Well, they probably weren't little anymore. Derek knew that he was nice enough to do it anyway, but, in Hector's eyes, waiting half an hour was part of his job.

When they reached the apartment, Nicole couldn't keep her hands off of him. The second the door closed, she pounced. He laughed and matched her eagerness. He pushed her body up against the wall and his hands explored all of her curves while he kissed her neck. He felt her tiny little waist as his hands roamed to her hips and back up to her breasts. He pulled down her dress and eased it over her hips until it fell to the floor. He scooped her up and carried her to the bedroom. She was pulling his shirt over his head and tugging at his pants as he laid her down. She didn't care if she ripped them; she wanted them off. Finally, she had him naked and he climbed over her. She pulled his head into hers for another kiss. She couldn't get enough of him and it was such a turn on. He loved how much they craved each other. When he was inside of her, she let out a sigh of relief, as if she had been waiting her whole life for his touch. He knew exactly how she felt. He, too, had waited his entire life to feel this way.

He wanted to make love to her tonight. He wanted it to be slow and sensuous. There were nights for fast and loud; this wasn't it. She had agreed to stay with him. He could stop counting the days he had left with her. He whispered to her about how much he loved her and how she had made him the luckiest man. He told her how he wanted to show her world. She replied back with sweet moans while she showed him what heaven must be like.

When they were resting afterwards in the glow of it all, he silently thanked her father for bringing her to him. Whether it was true or not, he liked the idea of it. He knew every night wouldn't be like this, but he loved that she would be there for all of them.

CHAPTER TWENTY-FIVE

Nicole woke up wrapped in Derek's arms. He must have opened up the wall to the balcony at some point, because she heard the ocean crashing into the beach before she opened her eyes. She couldn't believe how much her life had changed in less than two weeks. How was it even possible? She lost her father and had broken up with Andrew. Now she would be an ex-pat living on resorts all over the world.

With that thought, she realized that she needed to give her resignation at work. There was no need for someone to write remotely for a Chicago-based magazine. Then she thought again. This lifestyle she had now could open up so many possibilities. What if she offered to write about vacation options for Chicagoans to escape the cold and snow in the winter months? It wouldn't be weddings anymore, but there could be a captive audience for an article like that. She could focus on areas where she and Derek were staying and write an in-depth review of the area. She'd recommend his resorts, of course. That would be a win/win situation for the both of them. She needed to call her editor and suggest the switch. If he wasn't receptive to the idea, then she would simply resign her position. Still, she hoped he would consider it.

As she laid there thinking about everything with work, Derek began to stir. She turned her body into him. It still astounded her how handsome he was. His features were so rugged yet perfect. Before he opened his eyes, he somehow found her lips for a quick morning kiss.

"Good morning, love," he said in the middle of a yawn.

"Good morning to you," she said with a smile.

"How about having breakfast where the King's Head Pub used to be and then be off on our adventure?"

Nicole loved the idea. "Definitely," she said excitedly, "Also, let's take the bus to Mismaloya. That's how my dad always got there." She was glad that she was telling, rather than asking. She didn't want to start the relationship with Derek thinking he'd get to make all of the decisions. She wanted this relationship to work and that would be an important dynamic to figure out.

"Sure, just because you can travel by private jet now doesn't mean you're too good for the bus," he joked with her.

Did he really say jet? "You have a plane? Are you kidding me?" she laughed.

"I guess I'm not used to mentioning that with the ladies. Yes, you have a plane at your disposal. I can send it for your friends as well. Make sure to tell Kate that she can visit anytime she wants. She won't need to pay for a flight."

Nicole could barely wrap her head around that idea. That fact alone made it even easier to stay with Derek. She could have her friends here whenever they could come. "Give her a suite to stay in and she'll be here every weekend," she said, half-joking, half-waiting for the answer so that she could pass along the good news to Kate.

"We'll book her the best room in the resorts." He kissed her again and got up out of bed. For a second, she could barely breathe. Kate was going to lose it and

Nicole couldn't wait to tell her. She would honestly love Derek no matter what (she had loved the man when she thought he lived in Detroit, of all places), but this was a really fun perk to find out about.

Nicole was so excited to focus on her dad for the day that they were ready in no time. They each dressed for the beach, with tennis shoes for comfort, and headed to breakfast. Since the restaurant was close and they were taking the bus, there was no need for Hector drive to them.

The restaurant was just down the street from the hotel. It was no wonder her father had stumbled upon it one day. It was tiny as well. As they walked in the door, Derek began to tell her how it was set up when her father frequented it. The walls were now brightly colored, but he explained that it used to be almost all wood in order to resemble an English pub. Along the wall were three bar tables, oversized for the space. Now, five little white tables were in their place. The bar was located along the wall across from them. Derek said the size of the room hadn't changed and Nicole couldn't believe there was even space for a bar. Now, it had more dining tables and a wait staff area for drinks and supplies. There was a little register in the corner. She could see just slightly into the kitchen and imagined that's where the pub food was prepared.

While Derek found them a table, she tried to imagine everything as her father saw it. She sat down and closed her eyes, trying to see if she could feel his presence. She wasn't sure. She liked being there; it had a welcoming feel to it. She wondered if that was her dad. For once, Derek wasn't on a first name basis with the employees. She figured it was because he had breakfast in his apartment most days. Derek ordered an omelet and Nicole chose a breakfast burrito and they both had a latte. Her breakfast was fabulous. The pico de gallo tasted so fresh that it had to have been prepared just moments ago. She savored every bite.

When they finished, Nicole was happy to see that there was a bus stop right in front of the hotels. She knew that must be the stop her dad took. It made her smile as they waited. Derek must have noticed, because he put his arm around her and kissed her head. "Thank you for letting me be a part of this," he whispered into her ear, "I wish I could have met him. I would have told him that his daughter will always be loved and cared for."

With that, Nicole was ready to cry. She fought back the tears and just leaned her body into him as a thank you. She hadn't really put it together that her father had to die for her to meet Derek. Could the universe really have sacrificed her dad in order to make a chance encounter happen? She wasn't sure how she felt about the idea. She liked the idea that when her father died, he pulled some strings to have their paths cross. Not the other way around. He truly would have loved Derek. She couldn't imagine that he could have hand-picked another man that was more suited for her. They would have drunk beers together and discussed business. She pictured them up till all hours of the night talking, just as she could with Derek.

Luckily, the bus arrived to pull her away from her thoughts. She wasn't really sure what to expect, but it was nice, cute and clean. Derek paid the fare with coins and they sat down in the first available row of seats. The bus was about half-full of mothers with their children and a few men that looked like they were construction workers. There was an older woman who appeared to have bought a few things at the market. Now that she knew to some extent how wealthy Derek was, Nicole was surprised that he didn't look out of place. He fit right in. There wasn't a pretentious bone in his body and she loved that. Andrew would have stuck out like a sore thumb.

She needed to stop comparing him to Andrew. That relationship was officially over now. Derek was her future.

The bus ride to the Conches Chinas beach took about half an hour. Their stop was right next to a large outdoor bar and restaurant. Immediately, she felt like she could see her dad hanging out at the bar, having a shot of tequila. She was beginning to feel like an alcoholic with all of the day drinking, but a shot of tequila with Derek was exactly what she wanted just then. As if he could read her mind, he grabbed her hand.

"Let's do a shot for your dad."

"You do know me, don't you?" Nicole said with a laugh and they walked towards the bar. "I still have some of the seashells he brought me back from this very beach," she said. She wondered if there was something special she could do to display them.

"We'll have to get those and keep them with us wherever we stay," Derek said thoughtfully.

"What are we going to do about my stuff?" Nicole asked, realizing that she hadn't even thought about that.

"I already told Andrew that I would have your things sent to Kate's, but we can have them put in a storage unit and take a trip there to go through everything. I do travel light between places, but I have some meaningful items in some of the apartments I visit most often. I understand if there are things, like the shells, that you'd like to bring to each place."

"Thank you. There are some things of both my mother's and father's that I'd love to have."

"I'm going to ask Gael to meet tonight. I'll try to plan a face-to-face meeting with the people in Chicago soon and we can take care of both things. I want to meet Kate and any of your other friends as well."

Nicole started laughing at the idea of them meeting. "She'll be so excited. She already searched you on the Internet. I forgot about that. I want to see you back in your fighting days. I'm trying to picture you fifteen years younger."

"Imagine less grey," he said bluntly, giving her a smile.

"It's really not fair that men look better when they grey and women just look old," she responded with a playful scowl.

"I will love every grey hair on your head," he said and kissed her.

They took their shots of tequila and ordered beers to take out onto the beach. They walked together and Derek asked to hear more stories about her father while they searched for shells to keep. While they inspected shells, Derek told her that the name of the beach roughly translated to "Chinese Sea Shells". They were beautiful- brightly colored and larger than any she'd seen on beaches before. Most of the ones they found were smaller than the ones her dad had brought her. He must have waited to bring back the rare ones.

Derek did come across a beautiful shell and they both decided that it would be perfect to add to her collection. She could tell that he didn't want to invade on her collection from her father, but she wanted to add it because of the meaning of their trip to the beach. Despite his broken family life, Derek really seemed to understand the importance of it.

They stayed at the beach for the rest of the morning, relaxing in the sun. As they both lay quietly, Derek sat up and looked at the shoes they both had abandoned in the sand. Out of nowhere, he said, "Hey, we both have running shoes. Do you wanna take a run on one of your father's favorite beaches?"

"That's a great idea," her eyes widened at the thought. "With all of this eating and drinking, I could use a run."

They quickly put on their shoes and Nicole could tell she was already trying to get hers on faster. Oh Lord, Derek was going to find out how competitive she was. She usually tried to keep it in check, but somehow it always reared its ugly head. Maybe he'd like that about her. So far, chess was the closest thing they've come to competition and she knew she was out of her league there. But this could be different. She was pretty fast. *And not just for a girl*, she thought.

She hopped up before he did and started jumping in place. "Ok, mister, what's taking you so long? Let's do this."

He looked up from his shoes with his eyebrow raised and she knew he could already see it in her. Luckily, he was smiling, so that helped. "You think you can take me, love? Well, it's on." And he took off in a full sprint.

That was below the belt, she thought as she laughed and raced after him. Was the man good at everything?

Still, Nicole was fast and caught up rather quickly. Derek may have slowed down, but she preferred the idea that she was quicker. When she was next to him, she saw how hard he had been laughing and they both slowed to a reasonable pace.

Nicole was with her favorite person, doing one of her favorite things, on her father's favorite beach. She wanted to remember this feeling forever.

As they ran and talked, she couldn't help occasionally trying to gain a small lead. Every time she did, she could hear him laughing at her. Fortunately, he thought this competitiveness was an endearing quality thus far. They agreed on a halfway point and turned back to toward the restaurant on the beach. This was just what she needed and somehow Derek knew.

When they made it back, they stripped off their shoes and dove into the water to cool off.

"I'm hungry after that," Nicole said, relaxed in the cool ocean.

"Let's eat," was all he said and took her hand and they walked back onto the beach.

Nicole was disappointed to find out that the restaurant on the water they had visited a few nights before was not open for lunch. It was on their bus route back to the Romantic Zone. They decided to get something to eat at the restaurant in Conche Chinas. It was not their best meal, but it served its purpose.

On the bus ride home, they were a bit drained from the sun, but she was excited to mark off something else on the list of her father's favorites. They took the bus through the Romantic Zone and onto the Malecon.

Her father wasn't a religious person, but he always told her that he felt close to God in The Church of Our

Lady of Guadalupe. It was in the center of town and felt a million years old. Its tower seemed iconic. Whenever she had seen pictures of Puerto Vallarta, she hadn't realized that it was the church that stretched up above the little sky line of the city.

Derek held the large heavy door for her and she saw a collection box just inside. As she went to open her purse, to look for money Derek stopped her. "Allow me, love." He took out what had to be a large amount of pesos and slipped the folded stack into the collection box. He didn't even bother to count it. The gesture meant so much to her. Nicole wasn't a religious person and she wasn't Catholic, but, like her father, she did feel closer to God in such a beautiful place.

The walls were white and scalloped at the ceiling. There were large columns and gold trim everywhere. The floors were a gorgeous marble that could easily have been brought over from Italy. The wooden pews looked like they were made from the most magnificent trees. The altar itself was adorned entirely in gold. Nicole sat down in a pew and scooted down far enough for Derek to sit next to her. He rested his arm on the pew behind her and sat in silence. Nicole immediately wanted to visit some of the famous churches in Chicago. She felt bad that she never had before. She didn't even know the denomination of the church that she passed on Michigan Avenue all the time. What if she had walked pass such a gorgeous place all the time and never realized the beauty that was inside? Her dad had told her this is where he would come to think. She could see why. She was ready to ponder the reason for existence.

Derek didn't say a word to her while they were inside. He was letting her have her moment. They stayed maybe twenty minutes. Nicole remembered times with her father. She thought of times when she was a little girl and they'd play at the park. She remembered crying together when her mother was very sick. They were both so helpless; they couldn't do anything to make her better. She looked over at the empty part of the pew next to her and wondered if her parents were sitting there. She liked the thought of them together. Bill had his true love back and maybe they worked together to bring her to Derek. She felt a little sad that it hadn't occurred to her that her mother had taken a part in the plan. Maybe it was because Derek was so similar to her father that she thought he had chosen him. But her mother chose her father, so it would make sense that she helped find Derek as well. She was glad she had this time to work through that idea. It made her smile.

She leaned over to Derek because she felt the need to whisper. "Let's go," she said.

Wordlessly, he took her hand and they walked back out into the bright sun. She loved sharing that time with him. Of everything that day, having Derek sit next to her in the church had the biggest impact on her. Something about him solidified inside of her.

The next day, they wandered through the Romantic Zone on their way toward the Malecon. She wanted to find the little jewelry store where her father would bring her charms for her bracelet. She still had the bracelet in her jewelry box, which had filled up more with each of his trips to Vallarta.

First, she and Derek had another little restaurant to visit. The restaurant served authentic Mexican food and they had her father's favorite fajitas. It sat on a corner and was only large enough to hold eight tables and a small bar big enough for five bar stools. It was outside, with a trellis to enclose the area from the street. The kitchen behind the bar was inside a small building. Nicole was hungry, yet again. She couldn't wait to try the fajitas. They sat down at the bar and waited for the bartender to appear from the kitchen.

Derek started looking at the wall and began to laugh with surprise.

"Come and check out all of these pictures." He motioned for Nicole to look at the wall. "I had forgotten about this. A few years back, they took a picture of me with a guy I chatted with all afternoon. Look, they have pictures of guests all along the wall."

Nicole glanced over and saw a wall covered with photos of guests dining and drinking. They ranged from old tattered prints to glossy new ones, all showing families and friends, raising their glasses arm-in-arm, sitting in this very restaurant. She leaned in closer, excited to see a picture of Derek on the wall.

As it came into focus, her heart leapt from her chest and she found she couldn't breathe. She sat there and stared at her boyfriend, lifting his beer with her father. Bill was leaned toward Derek with his arm on the younger man's shoulder. He had a huge smile on his face. Tears instantly began falling down her cheeks.

"He looks so happy," she whispered through deep breaths as she tried to keep it together.

Still lost in looking at the pictures, Derek hadn't noticed Nicole's reaction. "Yes, I was. It was a great day. That old guy had some amazing stories to tell. He even gave me business advice," he said with a smile, remembering. Then he turned to face her and seemed to figure it all out. "Are you telling me...It can't be!" It was like he couldn't quite grasp onto a complete thought in his head. His eyes widened even more, if that was even possible, and he said, "You're the daughter!"

Nicole smiled as he wiped away her tears, "You met him! Nothing could be more perfect."

"I did, love, and he was such an interesting man. He was very proud of you. He went on and on about your intelligence and maturity. Even then, I could see how much he loved you. I never realized that you have his eyes."

She stood up and threw her arms around him. They stayed quiet for a few minutes. She had desperately wanted her father to meet Derek and now she knew he had. After she had collected herself, she sat back on her barstool. The bartender decided to approach them and Derek pointed to the picture. "What will it take to get this picture?"

"*Por qué, amigo?*" the bartender asked.

"This picture is of her father and me and we'd like to take it home and frame it."

"*Sí*, of course, friend," he smiled.

Derek carefully loosened the staple from the wall and removed the picture. When he handed it to Nicole, she looked at her father smiling and touched his face with her fingers. She smiled and a final tear appeared. She kissed his face in the picture and slipped it into her purse. "I don't want to risk ruining this. It's my most prized possession now."

They stayed at the bar for an hour or so, talking about every detail that Derek could remember about that day. They shared her father's favorite beef fajitas with poblano peppers. The bartender came out of the kitchen with a camera and asked to take their picture to fill the open space on the wall. Nicole stood in front of Derek and leaned back into his chest. He wrapped his arms around her and they both smiled for the camera.

Nicole was in a bit of a daze when they walked back out onto the sidewalk. She still couldn't wrap her head around the fact that Derek and her father had met. Derek took her hand. "The universe works in mysterious ways, love." How did he always know what she was thinking?

"It does," she agreed.

They made their way to the Malecon and began window shopping. "I hope the jewelry store is still open," she said.

"I already checked to make sure and the owner is expecting us today," Derek replied and he led her in what had to be the direction of the store.

"Thanks. I'm hoping I can find another charm for my bracelet. Even though I don't wear it, I'd like to add one for Dad." She leaned into him. She loved doing this, but it was still difficult to process.

Within no time, they reached the entrance to the jewelry store. The place was tiny and cold from the air conditioning, with large jewelry cases in a big U shape around the edges of the space. There was just enough room to fit a few customers at a time. The jewelry actually looked rather expensive. Everywhere Nicole looked, she saw the sparkle of diamonds. She did see a small case to the right of the door that held the little charms that her father had brought back to her. She smiled when she saw them and tears welled up in her eyes again. Fighting them back, she walked over for a closer look.

Derek walked over and spoke to the owner while Nicole looked through the options. She wasn't sure what she wanted, but hoped she would know it when she saw it. There were anchors and flowers and starfish. Many were focused on beach themes. That's not what she was looking for. Others looked like birth stones. She did see a few with baby themes. She already had many very similar to the selection there. And then she saw the perfect one- a thick silver charm with "Daddy's Little Girl" carved inside. She didn't have one like it yet and now it was exactly what she wanted.

"I'll take this one," she said out loud to whomever was listening. Both men walked over to her, Derek leaning over her shoulder to see what she had found.

"That's perfect, love," was all he said. Nicole leaned her body back into him in agreement.

"Can I show you something else as well?" he said sweetly.

"What did you find?" she asked.

"I've been speaking with this nice man and he has informed me that he has the best selection of diamonds in Puerto Vallarta. Plus, I thought that you would love to have an engagement ring from the same place your father shopped for you. What do you say?"

She stopped breathing for a second and stared at him. She couldn't think. She immediately knew in her heart that nothing would make her happier than being his wife, but she couldn't believe he had asked her the question.

He dropped down to one knee in the tiny little store where her father used to shop for her. "Will you marry me?"

She fell down on her knees as well and threw her arms around him. "Yes, Derek, I'll marry you!" she laughed and cried while she kissed him quickly on the lips. He hugged her tightly. They stayed there for a few moments and she was overwhelmed with the feeling that her mother and father were both there. It felt like their souls traveled through her body. She knew this was the right thing for her. Derek was her family now and all of a sudden, she felt completely whole again.

"Thank you, Derek. Thank you for doing this here. Thank you for thinking of my father." She was still crying.

He wiped away her tears and kissed each of her eyes tenderly. "I will work my entire life to only have tears of joy flow from those eyes. Now, come and pick out a ring."

They both stood and she was shaking as she looked into the case. She had barely noticed the owner before. He was a little old man with a face that had deep lines from a long life in the sun. He was short, with a full head of thick black hair and deep black eyes. He looked very kind. "I remember your father," he said in a raspy voice, "I will pack up your charm. Please allow it to be a wedding present for you. I will be back to show you any ring that you would like."

The tears began to form again. "Thank you," was all she could get out. Derek stood quietly next to her while she looked at her options. She had always loved the antique style of rings. It only took a moment to know which one should be on her finger and it wasn't at all what she would have expected. She was surprised how quickly she knew.

"This is the one," she pointed down at a beautiful diamond ring set in rose gold. She wasn't sure of the carat weight and couldn't care less, but guessed about two carats or so. It was surrounded by little diamonds, the rose gold prongs showing through each one. There were the same diamonds and rose gold along the entire band of the ring. The owner came over, opened the case, and handed Derek the ring. Nicole liked that touch; he got to slip it on her finger.

It fit perfectly without any sizing needed. "Once again, it's perfect," he said as he put it on her finger.

"Shall I wrap up the matching wedding band?" the owner asked.

"Of course," Derek said, "There's definitely going to be a wedding."

CHAPTER TWENTY-SIX

Derek was wiped out from the day in the sun. He glanced at the clock; they had been asleep for two hours. Nicole was still fast asleep. She was also naked, with only the ring sparkling on her finger, and it was the most beautiful sight. She really had chosen the perfect one. It represented her well, gorgeous and unique.

He was looking forward to his meeting with Gael that night. He was also happy that Gael and Nicole would get to be properly introduced. He remembered that they had only seen each other from across the room when Silvia was apprehended. He didn't want to be the type of husband that kept his wife in the dark about his business. He wanted Nicole to know as much as she'd like. He imagined her relaxing in the sun while he met Gael for poolside meetings. She may not care about any of it, but he was done hiding his life from everyone. He had found a woman to open up to. He didn't think they'd sit down and go through his financials, but he wanted her to know what she now had. He was ready to share all he had built.

He showered quickly to wake himself up and opened his computer to do a little work while Nicole was still sleeping. He sat on the couch, smiling as he saw the little Puerto Vallarta frame holding the picture with Old Bill and himself. Who would have guessed that man he had spent an afternoon with was actually Nicole's father?

But now it was time to focus on work. Derek reviewed some information and got his head together for his meeting. He made a list of questions he wanted to ask and things where he'd like further clarification. He had emailed quickly back and forth with the company heads about the Chicago property and they were ready for the next step. Gael was doing a great job and Derek was excited to see his interest in a larger role in the company. He printed out a few things he had been working on to see if Gael's brain thought the same as his. He wasn't testing him, more interested to see his thought process on choosing locations. He'd like to have things in motion when he took Nicole to Venice. He wanted to be able to leave his phone in the hotel room every day and not worry about work.

He heard her stirring in the other room and loved the sound of someone being there. He wondered now how he had lived all those years alone. She walked into the living room wearing his robe, her eyes dreamy and her hair a tousled mess. She looked perfect. "How long did I sleep?" she asked with a yawn, "Feels like years."

"We both slept a couple of hours. I've only been up about an hour now." He closed his computer and motioned for her to come sit by him on the couch. Even with such long legs, she could somehow curl herself up into the tiniest little ball. "Are you happy?" he asked her.

"I'm the happiest I've ever been," she said sweetly, "Do we need to get ready for you to meet Gael?"

"I've been preparing for that. Would you like to swim in the rooftop pool? He will meet us up there. We can order some food."

"Yes and I'm starved," she smiled, "Do they have those quesadillas here as well?"

"We'll get some sent over; they're Gael's favorite too."

"Yum. Thank you." She gave him a quick kiss. "I'm going to run through the shower to wake up."

And then she was off. He laughed to himself at her excitement over the quesadillas. It was so nice that she loved to eat food. He figured that he couldn't be the only man that got tired of women pretending they weren't hungry or that a salad was enough. He had such a wonderful time with her last night, devouring everything in front of them.

Nicole came out wearing her little black bikini with the same little shorts. He remembered that she had packed pretty light. They were going to do some serious shopping. He wanted her to have endless options wherever they were staying. Derek enjoyed clothes. He loved looking casual, but he also didn't just grab anything. His clothes were bought or made to fit him well. Like other times before, their minds were on the same thing. "Think I can get Maria to do some shopping for me here? That woman has great taste," Nicole joked.

"You make everything look good, love." He walked to meet her in the kitchen area. "But we will go shopping tomorrow if you'd like."

"Thanks. Since I'll be staying, I am going to need a few more things."

Yes, she would. "Let's go upstairs," he said, "you still haven't seen it yet."

He took her hand and they left the apartment. The sun had set while they slept and the Paraíso was tall enough to see quite a bit of the Romantic Zone from the rooftop. The streets were full of people walking and shopping and tables full of diners spilled out from little restaurants.

The rooftop was beautiful. There was a large pool that took up a majority of the space, going right up to the edge of the building, with a wrought iron railing around it. Large potted plants added to the outdoor feel. Along the side of the pool was a row of lounge chairs for guests to lounge and sun themselves during the day. Past those were a few cocktail-style tables and a small bar. Luckily, they were the only guests up there tonight and Derek didn't need to worry about speaking freely.

The bartender came by and Nicole ordered only water. They had been doing some serious drinking over the past two weeks. She was technically on vacation before. As of today, she was now living here. Derek liked that she seemed to change her mindset. Maybe he was way off, but it felt like she was settling into her life and most likely she didn't drink like a fish at home every day. Derek didn't either. He'd maybe have a beer or a glass of wine, but he mostly drank more when he was entertaining a woman on vacation. He ordered himself and Gael each a beer and a shot of tequila. He knew that, with the conversation he'd like to have, a shot would be in order. Just as everything was brought to the table, Gael arrived.

Derek properly introduced Nicole to Gael as his fiancé. She was adorable as she held out her finger to show him the ring, a giddy smile on her face. Gael's face lit up with a huge smile in return. He kissed Nicole's cheek and gave Derek a hug so big, it practically lifted him off the ground. *"Amigo,* I am so happy for you. You have been waiting a long time to meet her." He shook his hand and sat down. "Shall we take a shot?"

"I had those brought out for something else, but this seems like a time to celebrate." And they both threw back the tequila. "Sit, let's talk," he told Gael.

Derek began by asking his questions about the current project with the Chicago office. Gael did a great job of getting him up to speed on the situation. Derek handed him three folders of information he had just printed out at the apartment. "Take a quick look. Which location would you choose?"

Gael looked a bit confused, but picked up the first folder. Each one held information on options for Derek's next land purchase. The information included what Derek would use to make his decision. Although his gut instinct came into play quite often, the facts were important. He was interested to see if Gael would make the same decision. Gael rapidly reviewed data for Isla Mujeres, Todos Santos, and Riviera Nayarit, each of them an area in Mexico that could turn into a highly sought after vacation spot.

Quickly, Gael answered, "With only a few minutes to review, I'd choose Todos Santos." He smiled at Derek.

"Great job, my friend, very well done," Derek laughed, "We will move on that next."

Derek began to explain his ideas for the company. He asked Gael if he was interested in taking on a partnership role. He would begin taking on more responsibility in the selection of land options, first in cities that he and Derek chose together and then, ultimately, without Derek's assistance. When Gael agreed to the idea, they took another shot in celebration.

Derek enjoyed watching Nicole read by the pool while he discussed business. He could definitely get used to this set up. He felt great knowing that he could take a bit of a step back from business and enjoy life with Nicole. He knew she wanted to write, which would give him plenty of time to work. He wanted her to pursue her passion.

He discussed their plan of her writing about destination weddings on their properties with Gael, who thought it was an interesting suggestion as well. With Derek's own wedding coming up, he offered to contact a few locations and see if they were receptive to the idea.

When they concluded their conversation and had enjoyed their food, Gael said his goodbyes. He congratulated them both again and, though the wedding would be small, Derek knew that Nicole would want Kate as a maid of honor and he would ask Gael to be the best man. He still worked closely with Roger, but their relationship stayed far more on the business side of things. After working so closely with him, he had become a true friend. They didn't always agree, but in those times, he even felt like a brother. Derek was excited for this next step in their relationship, as well as his and Nicole's.

Derek and Nicole went back down to the apartment. Nicole hadn't called Kate yet and was dying to tell her the news.

"When should we have the wedding?" she asked.

"I would make you my wife right now. But we can have it as quickly as you like. Would you like to get married in Chicago?"

"No, I think we should have it on the beach at Playa Vallarta," she smiled, "Could we send that plane of yours for a few friends? How many does it hold?"

"Maximum capacity is ten passengers and we can always send it back for more. Maybe you'd like a few friends to come out early?"

Derek laughed as she started jumping up and down. He loved making her happy. He could tell that everything he had was such a surprise that it really never figured into how she loved him. That had been his biggest fear and why he had been so secretive in his past. Deep down, Derek hungered for true love. He hadn't gotten it from his mother; he wanted it from a wife.

Nicole was already on the phone with Kate and he sat on the couch, listening to her tell the story. He closed his eyes and relived it right along with her. She sounded genuinely happy and that gave him a sense of peace he had never experienced before. He could tell she was fighting back tears of joy again as she told Kate about finding the picture of him with her father. Then she must have reached the part about his plane, because he heard her start laughing loudly, "A plane, Kate. He has a plane. You can come whenever you want. You can stay at the resorts for free as well. We can still see each other all the time." Her excitement made him laugh again.

He began to wonder when they would get married. He meant it when he said he'd do it tonight. Weddings could get put together at the hotel in no time at all. Since Playa Vallarta was a smaller hotel, it didn't usually bring in weddings and they shouldn't have to worry about it being booked. They could have the ceremony on the beach and the reception in the open air lobby and bar. It would be perfect. Very important things in his life happened at that bar and now it would be the venue for his wedding reception. And, even with everything that had happened over the past few days with Silvia and Andrew, it was still her father's favorite place and he knew how much that meant to her.

CHAPTER TWENTY-SEVEN

The next morning, Nicole had just gotten off the phone with her boss Nathan. He was very happy for her and even told her that she could write her final column on her very own wedding. With all of the weddings that she had written about, writing about hers hadn't crossed her mind. Now that Nathan had put the idea in her head, she was extremely excited to write about it.

The preparation would take no time at all. She didn't need to interview anyone this time. She didn't need to learn the dynamics of the relationship. She was living it. Still, she was going to ask to borrow Derek's laptop for a little bit today and get down some ideas that were already flowing in her head. There had to be a store in Puerto Vallarta that sold computers. Nicole had some money saved and, though Derek would want to buy it, she really wanted to get set up herself. She'd need a light-weight computer and bag with all of the traveling they'd be doing.

Nathan also said he'd pitch her idea for travel destination spots. He asked her to write up a mock article after the wedding, to show in his meeting. He thought that even if it didn't get a regular column, they could buy her stories from time to time, especially going into the colder months of the year. Since she did want to write a book and would maybe write for Derek's properties, she wasn't sure she'd want a regular deadline anyway. Once a quarter might be nice.

Everything was falling into place. Nicole wasn't naïve enough to think that everything should come easy in life. If you want something, you needed to work and fight for it. But she didn't think it should be like that with love. Of course, relationships took work and you couldn't get too complacent, but at the same time, it should be easy to live and love together. All the stars were aligning and it seemed like a good sign.

Derek was sitting outside on the balcony when she came out of the bedroom. He was enjoying the view, his legs up on the table in front of him with one crossed casually over the other and a cup of coffee in hand. Nicole looked down at her ring for the millionth time that day. Her life felt surreal. She loved that man out there more than she ever thought possible. She wanted the wedding to be soon, too. She wanted to be Mrs. Derek Stone.

She grabbed her sunglasses and sat down at the table next to him.

"How did it go?" he asked.

"Great! He'd like me to write my final column on our wedding," she smiled at him, "He also said I could send him a mock story about Puerto Vallarta as an idea to still contract with them occasionally. I pitched him the idea of writing for travel ideas to escape the Chicago cold."

"That's great! I'm very proud of you and I can't wait to read about our wedding." He leaned over and kissed her lips quickly.

He listened while she filled him in on the phone conversation. When she finished and leaned back to soak up the sunlight, she felt him hold her hand. "How about going to Venice for our honeymoon?"

At the word "Venice", she jumped up in her seat. He was really going to take her to Venice? It had always been her dream to go there. Again, she felt like she couldn't breathe. "Really?"

"Yes, I'm thinking we spend a few weeks there. We could visit all over Italy after that if you'd like."

She dove out of her chair and landed on Derek's lap, laughing and kissing him all over. He took her face in his hands and she reached up to put her hands over his. She saw him notice her ring; he leaned in and kissed it. Then he took her mouth with his and her body seemed to melt into his. Luckily, she was already sitting on him because this kiss would have made her knees buckle from her own weight.

He reached back with one hand and grabbed ahold of her hair at the top of her neck. He tugged her head back hard, but seductively, and kissed all along her neck. She held on tight to his strong shoulders. She moved her hands over his chest, loving the feel of his muscles. She turned her body toward him, positioning herself so that her legs were now on each side of him. She could feel him getting hard below her and she used her body to urge him on. She was wearing a short sundress from her limited supply of clothing and he moved his hands to her thighs and slid them under the material to her hips.

He pushed her body deeper into him. Then, with one easy tug of the lace, he ripped the side of her panties and pulled them away from her. She laughed at the thrill it gave her. Nicole immediately began tugging his board shorts down low enough to free his hard erection. She climbed on top of him. There in the morning sun, on the balcony of her apartment that she shared with her fiancé, she rode him until he made her body lose control.

When she could see that he was about to cum himself, she leaned in close to him and whispered without thinking, "Stay inside me." She was surprised at herself. Maybe it was because she knew they would be married, but she didn't want to fear pregnancy anymore. When it happened, it would be the right time. He pulled her face in for another deep kiss and she felt all of his tension release underneath her. She smiled sweetly at him. "Let's go take a shower."

...

The next few weeks were a whirlwind until finally, Kate was to arrive. Nicole had spent the entire time shopping and working with a wedding coordinator and the Playa Vallarta to plan her small, intimate wedding ceremony and reception. Now she was pacing the airport arrivals area, waiting for Kate to walk through the doors. Crowds of people passed as commercial airlines landed and unloaded. Kate was the only passenger on her flight, so she would most likely arrive alone. Nicole thought it was funny that Kate saw the inside of Derek's plane before she did herself. She really wanted to fly to Chicago and do the round trip to pick Kate up, but she had so much to finalize for the wedding.

It felt like a wet sauna in the waiting area, just still air with no circulation. Nicole was hot and sticky. Her hair was sticking to her neck and she was beginning to get anxious. What if something had happened to the plane? Finally, she saw Kate come through the door and she raced to her as fast as she could. She had her best friend now; all was right with the world. Kate immediately grabbed her hand to see the ring and they laughed and screamed and hugged again. Nicole had never seen Kate like this and she loved it.

Derek had been staying in the background to give them their time. After they finished their hellos, Nicole called for him to come over. Kate squeezed her hand as he walked up and communicated silently to her that she thought he was as gorgeous as Nicole had said.

"Kate, it is wonderful to finally meet you," he said, "Nicole has been beside herself with excitement." Without asking, he went in for a hug.

"Thank you for flying me here. I could get used to traveling like that. Nicole, you've gotta try it sometime," she teased.

The three of them made their way to the car waiting for them outside. Derek had rented a larger SUV for Hector to drive until after the wedding, telling Nicole that he wanted there to be enough room for the extra passenger. He had also set up a car service to help with the added guests that the plane would bring in the day before the wedding. They would be too busy with the event itself for trips to the airport. She loved that he was taking care of all the little details so that she wouldn't be stressed.

Kate was in awe of their apartment. She had the same reaction that Nicole did the first time she saw it. As they sat out on the balcony the first night, she agreed with Nicole that her life was surreal. She never came across as jealous. That wasn't Kate's style. She was truly happy for her.

Nicole did worry that she was a bit jaded about relationships from her career. Dealing with unhappy and broken couples as a divorce lawyer had turned her into a bit of a cynic. Nicole didn't blame her; it could happen to anyone. But Nicole did worry that she wouldn't find happiness with a man until she could see past all that. It would take the right man for that to happen. She hoped Kate found him soon. She wanted happiness for everyone in the world now, especially her best friend.

They talked and drank bottles of wine all night. Derek had arranged for Kate to stay in the hotel room next to their apartment. That way, she could stumble next door to fall asleep. Once they said their goodbyes and Nicole and Derek both watched Kate enter her hotel room, he scooped up Nicole and carried her tired body into the bedroom, laying her down for bed. She curled into his body and was asleep in moments.

The next morning, Hector drove Nicole and Kate into the Malecon so that they could shop for her wedding dress. She was determined to wait for Kate to find it. She wouldn't have her mom there, so she wanted memories with Kate. There were a few shops off the main drag that most tourists would wander past. Nicole was no longer a tourist now. She was a local, at least for the time they'd live there.

The first shop was tiny and hot. It was so dark that the two women could barely see the dresses. The little old shopkeeper seemed like she was ready to put a curse on them when they'd giggle about something. They couldn't get out of there fast enough.

The second place she heard about was just what they were looking for. It was still a tiny shop, but it was bright and cheery and the woman that ran it was young and gorgeous, inviting and earnest. Kate joked that if she modeled the dresses, she would sell out of inventory. She introduced herself as Lupe and handed them each a glass of wine. She told them to enjoy themselves and have fun. Nicole tried on loads of dresses and Lupe convinced Kate to try on a few for fun. This was exactly what Nicole had hoped for.

Ultimately, Nicole decided on two dresses. The first, for the ceremony, was strapless and long. The material was light and airy and it cinched around her mid-drift to show off her figure. Then she fell in love with a shorter dress and Kate was determined that Nicole needed it for the reception. It was sleeveless and extremely short, with an added sheer layer of material that fell at an angle that ended almost at her knees. Her favorite part was a ruffle of material that dropped at an angle in the back to represent a train. It only dropped to her knee, rather than behind her on the floor.

She and Kate spent the rest of the afternoon picking out the perfect dress for Kate and shoes and jewelry for both of them. They also decided to stop for a lunch and cocktail on Derek.

Derek had given Nicole a credit card with Nicole Stone embossed on the front of it as an early wedding present and told her to go have fun. Usually, such a thing would make her uncomfortable to go on a spending spree, but given it was for her wedding, she made an exception. She was going to have to get used to the fact that she didn't need to live on any kind of budget anymore. She didn't want to go crazy and turn into a shopping monster, but she liked the idea that if she wanted something, she could have it.

The night before the wedding, Nicole stayed in Kate's room. Derek offered to go to another room but Nicole wanted him to be comfortable in his own home. Besides, she would have fun with Kate in her room. It was like old times. Kate and Nicole promised to visit each other monthly. And Kate was thrilled to find out the likely possibility that Nicole and Derek would be living on a new property in downtown Chicago for part of the year. They agreed that the summer would be the most fun and joked that they should make sure Derek agreed with that decision. They stayed up later than they had planned, which was a bit of a concern. Nicole didn't want to have bags under her eyes for her wedding. But it was worth it. She would remember that night for the rest of her life.

And then the moment of truth arrived. She was standing at the edge of the beach, watching her friends from Chicago and Derek's friends and business acquaintances from Puerto Vallarta and Nuevo Vallarta mill around the chairs set up along the beach. Derek was standing by the altar with Gael and he looked incredibly handsome.

She looked down at her dress, hoping he'd feel the same way about her. How did she get so lucky? She was about to marry the man of her dreams. It was like a scene out of a movie. She wondered if her parents really could have had a role in orchestrating all of this. If so, they had pulled it off perfectly. She wanted her mother there, though she had become used to big moments in life without her. She hoped that didn't seem cold. It was probably a coping mechanism in life.

But her dad...she missed him so much in that moment. She wished he was there to walk her down the aisle to meet the man waiting for her. Then she felt his presence more than she ever had since he passed. She smiled and knew he was there. He would be walking with her, now and forever. Finally, it was time and she began walking towards the man she loved so deeply and she thanked her father again for sending her Derek.

THE END

Thank you for reading *Love on the Malecon*! If you enjoyed it, please consider taking a moment to leave me a review at your favorite retailer. And don't forget to check out a sneak peek of my next novel, *Love on Ocean Drive*, at the end of this book!

Thanks!

Aubrey Parr

Acknowledgments

Thank you to my beta readers that gave me the reader's perspective while I wrote. I would like to give a special thank you to Kelly from For the Love of Books and Alcohol for your endless hours of help and support. You are an amazing mentor in this process and made *Love on the Malecon* what it is today.

Thank you to Allison for editing the book. My mind may be a little dirty at times, but so is my grammar.

Thank you to my mom for naming Love on the Malecon. Thank you for being the perfect combination of a supportive mother and a critical eye to help make the book its possible best. You are invaluable.

Thank you to my husband for inspiration in certain scenes. Wink, wink.

About the Author

Aubrey Parr waited until she was forty to publish her first novel. Although she received her Master's in Accounting, Aubrey always knew that she wanted to write. She was inspired by her great-uncle; author Evan S. Connell. With a few years of life experience under her belt she decided it was time. She lives with her husband and daughter outside of Chicago, Illinois. When she's not chasing after her daughter she sneaks off to create steamy stories of wonderful love affairs.

Connect with Me

Check out my website and sign up for my newsletter:
AubreyParrBooks.com
Friend me on Facebook:
http://facebook.com/aubreyparrbooks
Follow me on Instagram:
http://instagram.com/aubreyparrbooks
Follow me on Twitter:
http://twitter.com/aubreyparrbooks
Follow me on Pinterest:
http://pinterest.com/aubreyparrbooks
Follow me on Goodreads:
http://goodreads.com/aubreyparrbooks

<u>Love on Ocean Drive</u> Sneak Peek

CHAPTER ONE

You would think that Kate Olesen was used to flying on a personal jet by now, but she wasn't. Every time she walked into the luxurious cabin, it felt like a dream.

Her best friend Nicole had been married to her husband, Derek Stone, for almost a year now. And he came with a personal jet. Kate had spent the better part of the year visiting them in different resorts almost every month. Usually the Stones were in Mexico, but this time Kate didn't need her passport.

Kate had just landed in Miami and was in a cab, on her way to the hotel. The driver seemed to be in some kind of hurry, weaving in and out of traffic while they crossed the causeway to Miami Beach. It was making her sick. Even with the window down, the humidity took over. It was a million degrees inside the car. The cab driver was humming to salsa music that was playing far too loud. She wondered how bitchy she would feel if she still flew commercially. Kate didn't like it when she was crabby and for some reason, she was.

Well, she knew why she was. It was Ethan again. Somehow she had pulled off the "acting casual" thing far too well with him. Ethan seemed to see her as one of

238

the guys. They have worked together in the same law office for the past few years and he had immediately caught her attention. No matter how much she tried to ignore it, she had a thing for him, like a school girl with a crush. She didn't like feeling that way. She knew he liked her, but just not in the way she had hoped.

Usually that was okay with her. But some days were harder than others. Being a divorce attorney made her a little jaded about relationships and marriage. It really wasn't anything she was interested in at the moment, anyways. Her career was going great, she was on track to be a partner before she was forty, and that was what was important right now. She was married to her job and, so far, it was a great husband.

She leaned her head back on the seat and tried not to breathe in the smell of the cab. Maybe that was her problem. Maybe once she was able to get out of this little sweat box she would be fine. She realized there were a lot of maybes going through her mind at the moment. Soon she would be in Miami Beach with her best friend and all would be right with the world. Although she had traveled far more lately than she ever had before, for some reason, it really felt like she needed this weekend away.

By the time Kate opened her eyes, they were in the South Beach area on Ocean Drive. She checked out all of the hotels, each with outdoor restaurant seating in front. She could see endless couples and groups of friends drinking and enjoying lunch. It was a gorgeous day, the sun shining bright. She was already feeling better.

Kate remembered Nicole telling her that they chose a site that was a block inland. Nicole and Derek had stayed at a hotel on Ocean Drive during one of his investigative visits and they barely slept with the music playing till all hours of the morning. Derek knew that his clients would not have wanted that for their guests. The location he found was perfect. It was in the middle of South Beach; one block's walk from the excitement, but far enough to provide a quiet night's sleep. Collins Avenue had far more stores than bars and the hotels had smaller bars with coffee shops, rather than a party atmosphere.

The cab driver pulled up to the Ocean Azul Hotel and Kate immediately relaxed. She grabbed her overnight bag next to her, (she had become an expert packer), stepped out onto the sidewalk, and looked up at the hotel. It was perfect.

It had a beachy chic look- stark white with blocks of blue in different parts of the building. The name Ocean Azul was written in a bright turquoise blue vertically down the front. There was a small bar and restaurant in front, with tables on either side of the entryway. Kate loved it.

After scanning the little hotel, she saw Nicole and Derek sitting in the table closest to the door. They looked deep in conversation and didn't appear to have noticed she had arrived. Then again, it looked like they didn't notice anyone else around them either. That's how it had been since they met. Deep down, Kate hoped that one day she may be lucky enough to find a love like that.

She walked right up to the table and didn't get their attention until she sat down next to Nicole. They screamed at each other and hugged, like they always did. Derek got up and gave her a welcoming hug as well. Nicole was relieved to finally have her there. She loved their monthly weekend visits and she was excited for her to see the hotel.

"How was the flight?" Nicole asked.

"That part was wonderful, as usual. The cab ride smelled like shit, but I'm glad to finally be here." Kate crunched her face at the memory of the cab ride and leaned back in her chair, excited for her mini vacation to begin. Derek hailed the server and ordered Kate a dirty martini without even asking. She loved that he had come to know her almost as well as his wife did.

"Thank you," she smiled at him. She really had come to love him like a brother.

"I'm going to leave you two to catch up," he returned the smile and wandered inside the hotel.

"What shall we do first?" Nicole asked, taking a drink of her wine. Just then, her martini arrived and Kate was ready to savor it.

"I don't think I've been here since college," Kate confessed. "I'm not sure what to do."

"Did you think about the tattoo idea? We could do that tonight." Nicole loved tattoos and Kate had always teetered on the edge of getting one. This time, she was prepared to do it.

"I did decide," she smiled, waiting for Nicole's response.

"Yes, finally! You can't back out now. What are you getting?" Nicole was ecstatic.

"I'll show you a picture." Kate pulled out her phone and opened it to a screenshot of a tattoo, a simple drawing of a little girl reaching for a red heart-shaped balloon.

"You have this on the wall of your apartment. What is it?" Nicole took the phone from her to get a better look.

"It's the Girl with Balloon stencil from Bansky, the street artist. I love that there can be so many interpretations. What does the balloon represent and is she reaching for it or releasing it? Depending on my mood, I see it differently. I'm thinking the inside of my wrist or the back of my shoulder. I have to think of work, after all."

Nicole wasn't surprised at Kate's choice. Kate had been an art history major in college, before she decided to change her major to pre-law and continue on to law school. Something to do with artwork did make sense.

"I love it. There's a tattoo shop Derek suggested just down the street."

"Great. I want to get into the room and take a quick shower and change." After that cab ride, Kate was a bit concerned that she could still notice that weird smell on her.

Nicole already had Kate's key. With their hotels and resorts, Kate never had to officially check into a room at the front desk. Nicole always had a key for her and the room was always huge and excessive for one person.

This was not any different. The door opened into a sitting area with a two comfortable chairs and a huge TV on the wall. There was a small wet bar with a small refrigerator and microwave. The fridge was always stocked with the tiny airplane-sized bottles of alcohol and somehow there was always a martini glass and shaker tin. Kate thought the personal touch was sweet. The sitting room opened up to a bedroom with a king bed, side tables, a dresser, and another large TV. The entire exterior wall was all windows, with sliding glass doors that accessed a balcony. The windows were already opened and she could hear the sound of people talking and eating from the sidewalk tables below.

Nicole grabbed the remote and sat down in a chair. "I'll wait for you to get ready." Since her trips were always just weekends, Nicole already knew she wouldn't want to waste time relaxing in the room. Kate turned on the shower and stared at herself in the mirror while she waited for the water to heat up. She noticed that flying in a private jet somehow made one look far less disheveled than commercial travel. She wondered why that was.

Kate was about 5'5" tall, with striking black hair around shoulder length and angled toward the front. She had dark brown eyes and a little button nose. Her mouth was big, with a wide smile that made everyone in a room want to know what she was so happy about. Her skin was fair enough that she always expected to return home from visits with a freckled nose.

She could see Nicole through the reflection in the mirror. She was sitting sideways in the big chair, her long legs flung over the arm rest. She loved that woman like a sister, but they looked absolutely nothing alike. Nicole was tall and tan with long blond hair. Kate never wished she was a blond though. She honestly liked the way she looked. That brought Ethan back to the front of her thoughts. Was that the problem? Was he into tall blondes? He seemed to genuinely like Kate, but maybe she wasn't his physical type. They laughed at work and hung out and had drinks with everyone. She just seemed to be stuck in the Friend Zone and she wasn't sure why.

She had never brought it up with him; that idea made her cringe. "Girl, you need to get laid," she said out loud to the reflection in the mirror.

"What babe?" Nicole asked loudly from the next room.

"Oh, just telling myself I need to get laid this weekend," Kate laughed. She would always tell Nicole anything. There was no reason to feel self-conscience with her.

Nicole practically spit out her water she was drinking. "We'll get right on that, honey," she called back to her.

Kate showered and put on some makeup. Being an attorney, she had to dress rather conservatively at work. She used these visits to have some fun with her clothes. Nicole was wearing a bright orange summer dress, so Kate chose a green backless number that came just above the knee and tied around her neck in a halter-style. There was a little bow at the base of her back. When she was ready, she came out and turned around to show Nicole.

"I love it," Nicole smiled at her.

"I'm thinking about the tattoo as well. If I decide on my shoulder, I figured this gave good access."

"Plus, you're bound to get laid wearing it," Nicole joked.

"Perfect. Let's go."

www.ingramcontent.com/pod-product-compliance
Lightning Source LLC
Chambersburg PA
CBHW051428170626
46809CB00006B/2363